D1744223

# The Foy
## and other folk tales

Best wishes

Laurence Tuddock

# The Foy
## and other folk tales

Lawrence Tulloch

The Shetland Times Ltd.
2006

The Foy and other folk tales

Copyright © Lawrence Tulloch, 2006.

ISBN-10 1 904746 23 3
ISBN-13 978 1 904746 23 2

First published 2006.

Cover design and all illustrations by Sheila Faichney

All rights reserved.
No part of this publication may be reproduced, stored in
a retrieval system or transmitted, in any form, by any means,
electronic, mechanical, photocopying, recording or otherwise,
without the prior written permission of the publishers.

A CIP catalogue record for this book is available from the British Library.

Printed and published by
The Shetland Times Ltd., Gremista, Lerwick,
Shetland ZE1 0PX, Scotland.

# Contents

# Preface

WHEN I was a child and growing up in the Haa of Midbrake in Cullivoe, Yell, in the 1940s and 50s, the way of life was very different to the way it is now. We had no mains electricity and no mains water. Of course there was no TV. The radio was powered by a combination of wet and dry batteries and therefore used very sparingly.

The BBC news was listened to twice a day, and very little else. Visitors were valued because they brought news and brightened the conversation. Visitors we had in plenty, and through them and my father I began to hear stories.

Among the regular visitors were brothers John, Robbie and Bertie Henderson, who lived in the most remote part of the island. There was no road to their home in West-A-Firth; they either had to cross in a boat or walk all the way around Gloup voe. Sometimes they would stay overnight.

In different ways they were the best storytellers that I ever heard. They could make the most mundane happening seem like a major event and the humour was brilliant. They had hearts of gold, always willing to give and to share anything they owned. They taught me a huge amount, especially John.

On John's knee I learned the art of avoiding the bones when eating fish. He showed me how to break lamb bones and how to extract the marrow, but I never summed up the courage to tell him that I did not like marrow. Eventually I acquired a taste for it, as well as a taste for sheep's heads and the eyes, the part, he said, that the crow would never give to its young.

Hearing them and others telling stories along with my father, I never fully appreciated, as a child, that I was hearing the very best. I believed that what I was hearing was routine and that everyone could tell stories equally well.

My father would never have described himself as a storyteller, nor would have known the phrase tradition bearer, but the fact was he told stories every day of his life and he was passionately interested in the bygone way of life and the Shetland dialect. Indeed, I wondered if I should write these stories in the dialect but, in the end, decided that they would appeal to a wider readership written in standard English.

It is not surprising that this collection of stories comes mostly from my father's telling. Many of them I learned when I was so young that I cannot remember when I first heard them. Latterly I have met many fine storytellers and shared stories with them, therefore adding to my store of tales.

Many of these stories are widely known and I do not claim that I ever have the definitive version. However, I have made an honest endeavour to pass on the stories the way I heard them. Some I have written myself while others are simply stories that I have heard and like.

I can never recreate the atmosphere of the Haa of Midbrake of more than half a century ago, nor can I bring back the storytellers of that time, but my memories are vivid and it is my hope that readers can share some of my love and enjoyment of the tradition that I was lucky enough to inherit.

*Lawrence M. Tulloch*

# Acknowledgements

IN COMPILING and writing this collection of stories I am grateful for the help of a great many people.

First and foremost my late father Tom. Not only was he the source of most of the tales but I inherited from him the love of stories.

Dr Donald Smith from the Scottish Storytellers Forum gave me my big break when he invited me to the Netherbow in Edinburgh to be part of the International Storytelling Festival in 1996. He has always encouraged me to write and very kindly read what I had done. I can never thank him enough.

Not only has Professor Bo Almqvist written an introduction but also over the years he has given me his friendship, help and advice. I do not believe that there is any such thing as a story that Bo does not know. At what he does he is, quite simply, the best.

A rare and precious event occurs when you meet someone that you can truly gel with, somone who is always on the same wavelength and someone that you love like a brother. Such a man is Tom Muir from Orkney. For me he brought a new dimension to storytelling in quality and delivery. The adventures that we have shared together, at home and abroad, are big highlights in my life.

Sheila Faichney so quickly agreed, to design a cover for the book and produce illustrations in her own very attractive style. Sheila has a lot to answer for because it was she who introduced me to Tom!

Another really close friend is Andy Ross. Not only is he a model neighbour but also one of the very few that I can rely on to constructively criticise my writing. Every opportunity that Andy gets to further the cause of storytelling, he takes. Tom Muir is one of many that he has invited to perform in that great venue, the Wind Dog Café.

Thanks also to Frances Gillham of Gloup. She read some of the first stories that I wrote for this book and always gave me positive feedback.

Sincere thanks to Charlotte Black and The Shetland Times Ltd. for so readily agreeing to publish *The Foy*. Without them it might never have seen the light of day.

# The Foy and other folk tales

~ ~ ~

Thanks to a new and delightful friend, Alexa Fitzgibbon from France for taking my photograph – no easy task!

Storytelling friends, too numerous to mention, from far and wide have contributed by inviting me to events and festivals in places as far apart as America and Sweden.

Last, but by no means least, I thank my family, wife Margaret and daughter Liz. Without them I would be nothing and nowhere. Their support and help is vital and, no matter what, they keep my feet firmly planted on the ground.

# Foreword

## From Still Rooms to Rolling Cabins

I WALKED into the Still Room of the Stromness Hotel, Orkney, that October evening in 2000, little knowing that my life would never be quite the same again.

A fire burned brightly in the hearth, and the small but dedicated band of enthusiasts huddled at the bar, like piglets around a sow. I joined them and ordered a pint.

I had been asked, by Sheila Faichney from the Orkney Tourist Board, to tell a couple of stories at a small storytelling festival she had put together in order to try to extend the tourist season.

Over by the wall sat the star of the evening's event, a stranger to me called Lawrence Tulloch. He came from Shetland and was the first professional storyteller that I had ever seen. I felt rather uncomfortable being around a professional, and felt it best to remain at the bar and not to push my way into his company. After all, I was only there to make up numbers and it was well known that I would work for whisky instead of hard cash.

Lawrence was his usual cool self as he performed, having a confidence about him that set everyone else at ease. His stories were spellbinding, full of life and humour that came straight from the heart. The audience were on good form, while a band sat in the corner and played traditional music between bouts of stories, adding to the merriment.

When it was my turn I did a couple of stories and then retired to the bar. Later I was invited to meet Lawrence, and I must confess to feeling a bit shy. I thought he would pity my feeble attempts to be a 'storyteller', but found him to be a charming and delightful man. Little did either of us know what fate had in store for the pair of us.

His recollections are a bit different. He saw me saunter in and head to the bar, ignoring him completely. He later said that he thought I was 'one of the Orkney intelligentsia' (although he has used more colourful and less flattering words to describe our first meeting when we are together). It was only after we got talking that he discovered shyness rather than arrogance directed my behaviour.

# The Foy and other folk tales

~ ~ ~

The following year Lawrence was the prime mover in getting me invited to the first Shetland Storytelling Festival. This brought me into contact with other storytellers, which helped me gain the experience that I lacked. It was at this time that I met Lawrence's wife Margaret, who remains, along with Lawrence, one of my favourite people on the planet. I also met their daughter Liz, as we had to carry a large fish-tank into her house as the new abode for her psychotic albino frog (who goes crazy during the full moon, but that's another story).

While in Shetland I met Davy Cooper, who would also play an important role in my life in the coming years, and George McPherson, the storyteller from Skye. It was he who invited Lawrence and I to his festival the following year, where we met a bus load of American tourists who enquired how many hours we spent practising together. They seemed amazed to hear that we didn't practice at all, yet alone practice together.

Another Shetland Festival brought another invite to our northerly neighbours, but things were moving in a direction that neither of us could have dreamed of.

I met Davy Cooper again in Foteviken in southern Sweden in August 2002. He was the representative of the Shetland Amenity Trust in a new EU funded project called 'Destination Viking: Sagalands', while I represented Orkney Museums and Heritage. This opportunity led to Lawrence and I getting together again in Orkney for a meeting, which resulted in an invitation to a storytelling festival in Iceland.

We decided to travel to Iceland in true Viking fashion; by sea. We sailed on the *Norröna* from Shetland to Faroe, then on to Iceland where we had to take a flight across the country to Reykjavik. After a short but highly enjoyable festival, which also featured our friends Bob Pegg and Heather Yule, Lawrence and I were taken over the mountain roads and around the north of the island by the organisers Jona, Ásta and her husband Joi.

Sagalands also gave us the opportunity to work together again in Örnsköldsvik in northern Sweden. Here we were taken for a ride on a snowmobile, a more sedate sleigh ride over a frozen lake, then to a reconstructed longhouse where we were fed rancid herring,

# Foreword

~ ~ ~

which was, as we Orcadians would say, 'no great'! As a gift from the local library that we had performed in we were given golf umbrellas, which we had to take home with us as hand luggage on the plane. This was during a period of heightened security because of terrorist attacks, and we had to show the officials the evil looking metal tip to our brollies and say feebly "It's alright; we're storytellers." It worked, we got them home!

We were invited to the International Storytelling Festival in Edinburgh in 2004. I had a good friend of ours with me, Hjorleifur Helgi Stefansson (my pet Viking from Iceland), who was Ásta's brother-in-law. He had been staying at my house brushing up on his storytelling skills, and I had brought him along to see other storytellers in action.

On the eve of our stint we had a few drams in the flat we had been given, and I looked at Lawrence, and with a nod of my head towards Hjorleifur I said, "Whit dae ya think?"

Lawrence nodded and said, "Aye!"

The following day (after getting Heather Yule's blessing) we told Donald Smith that we were hi-jacking his festival and that Hjorleifur was coming on with us too. Donald just laughed, and told us to carry on. It was quite a debut for the young Icelander.

That same year we did Bob Pegg's Highland Storytelling Festival, called 'Tales at Martinmas'. We had both taken part in it before, but this time we were together, which made it special. I was having problems with my sight, so Lawrence or Margaret acted as my 'eyes', a kindness that I appreciated very much.

In April 2005 we were invited to the island of Sandøy in Faroe to give training sessions to tour guides who wanted to use stories as part of their tours. We once more boarded the *Norröna* and were due to arrive in Torshavn around 5.00am, which meant being out of our cabins by 4.00am. As we approached Faroe (going from Shetland via Denmark), we were hit by a force nine gale which caused the ship to pitch up and down violently. It was a lucky break for us, as we got a lie-in, a free breakfast and rhythmically rocked to sleep courtesy of the North Atlantic. Our cabin was most unlike the 'Still Room' of the Stromness Hotel, as it certainly moved around plenty.

# The Foy and other folk tales

~ ~ ~

In November 2005 we travelled to Lewis, where the ferry from Ullapool was caught in a severe gale the day that we arrived. People on board were texting their loved ones to say goodbye, as they were convinced that the ship would sink. We arrived a bit late, but along with local storyteller Ian Steven we told stories to many primary school children.

I can honestly say that Lawrence Tulloch has had a huge impact on my life, both as a storyteller and as a friend. I have had the honour of being a guest in the lovely home that he and Margaret have in Yell, and we have had great fun telling stories in the Wind Dog Café that lies just a stone's throw away from it.

There have been times when I thought that my life was in danger through laughing too much, like the time I actually woke up during the night in fits of laughter after hearing a particularly amusing reminiscence of Lawrence's the previous day

Lawrence is a true friend who is there for you whether life is good or bad. He is a genuine human being, and this shines through in his stories. I was delighted when he said that he was writing down his stories, and greatly honoured when I was asked to write this foreword.

His stories are a pure slice of Shetland, and will bring joy to readers all over the world, regardless of their age.

To conclude I would say this: move over Hans Christian Andersen and the brothers Grimm, Lawrence Tulloch just rode into town!

*Tom Muir*

# Introduction

## Lawrence Tulloch and his Tales

THIS book, aptly entitled *The Foy* (a Shetland word for 'feast'), contains a selection of the best tales told by Lawrence Tulloch, one of Shetland's foremost storytellers.

My first meeting with Lawrence is a story in its own right. It took place on 1st July 1996 at about 2 o'clock. This was on my first visit to Shetland, where I had gone for the double purpose of familiarising myself with localities mentioned in the Old Icelandic *Orkneyinga saga* and attempting to obtain an overview of Shetland folklore.

I knew of Lawrence's existence, since I had been advised by the School of Scottish Studies in Edinburgh to go and see him. What I did not know, however, was that the man I saw standing in front of me outside the teashop in Gutcher, north Yell, should happen to be just him. Still ignorant of his identity, I addressed him by asking for the name of a small island that was lying in front of our eyes. He replied that it was called Lingy or Yella-Linga. This provoked the next question: "Wasn't that where the bear was?" I can still see the gleaming surprise in Lawrence's eyes as he exclaimed: "How do *you* know about the bear!?"

The bear in question was indeed an old acquaintance of mine; I first read about him in the writings of Jakob Jakobsen, the famous Faroese author of *The Etymological Dictionary of the Norn Language in Shetland*, and I had myself written about that self-same bear in my book *Viking Ale*. These pieces of information, however, I did not divulge to Lawrence. Instead, avoiding his question, I went on to ask if he would mind telling me the story. This he did without the slightest hesitation, still standing looking out over Yella-Linga. I am lucky enough to have this performance preserved on tape, since I hastened to switch on my portable tape recorder. Another telling of this remarkable story, *Jan Tait and the Bear* can be enjoyed in this book.

My enthusiasm over the Jan Tait story sufficed to convince Lawrence of my genuine interest in his tales. He invited me in to his house and there I recorded a string of stories, some of which, e.g. *Da*

# The Foy and other folk tales

~ ~ ~

*Oo Tiggers, The Selkie Boy of Breckon* and *The Minister and the Cow*, are also included in this collection.

I have since had the great pleasure of listening to Lawrence on numerous formal and informal story telling occasions at home in Shetland as well as abroad, in places ranging from Ireland to Iceland. On one of these occasions, in Orkney in January 2004, a heavy snowfall put a stop to all communications from Kirkwall, so we came to spend three days together, more or less snowed in, in the home of the Orkney storyteller Tom Muir. Words fail to give an impression of the seemingly endless stream of tales and yarns that flowed from Lawrence's mouth during these days – and nights.

One would, of course, be curious to know how Lawrence became a storyteller, and when, where and how he learned his tales. Fortunately, we are in a fairly good position to answer these questions, thanks to the valuable notes Lawrence himself has appended to his tales, and also to information provided by scholars who previously carried out folklore collecting in Shetland.

First and foremost, Lawrence is a bearer of a rich family legacy. Born in 1942 in Cullivoe, north Yell, an area saturated in folk tradition, he learned his tales from many relations of an older generation, both on his mother's and his father's side. The man who exercised by far the largest influence on him was his father, Tom Tulloch (1914-1982), whose traditions went back well over a hundred years to the time when the haaf fishing was still flourishing. Humble and modest as Tom was, he did not consider himself a storyteller, but he certainly must be termed one of the very best of that class in Shetland in his time, both in view of the many tales he knew and the masterly way in which he delivered them. Most fortunately, many of his stories were recorded in the 1970s under the auspices of the School of Scottish Studies by Alan Bruford. Much of this material also appeared in print in the journal *Tocher*, where (in issue no. 30) Tom's life story is also found. Interestingly, several of Tom's tales in print in *Tocher* are found in Lawrence's versions in this book. As a result of this we are often in the position to ascertain in minute detail how faithfully Lawrence preserved the treasure he inherited, although he has proved himself able to add to it and adapt it to conditions and situations encountered in our days.

# Introduction

~ ~ ~

But Lawrence's repertoire has roots outside the family tradition, as well. He was, from childhood and early youth, in close contact with men and women who told stories coming from all over north Yell and further afield in other parts of Shetland.

Lawrence learned tales outside Shetland too. These he learned at the many storytelling festivals and congresses he attended in a wide variety of places. Such tales include *The Denschman's Hadd*, which he learned in Orkney from Tom Muir; *The Gold Cradle*, learnt on the Isle of Skye from Marion Craig; and *The Red Roses*, told to him by a Faroese storyteller on Sandoy, Faroe Islands. The two last-mentioned tales, originally told in Scottish Gaelic and Faroese respectively, were translated orally at Lawrence's request. Apparently he knew them after hearing them only once.

Finally, not even satisfied with the myriad of stories he learned in all the manners described, Lawrence himself started to invent yarns, based on traditional themes or strange or comical experiences of his own. Examples of this are *Walkabout*, *St Patrick*, *The Trows' Boats* and *The Reverend's Ruin*.

From all this it is apparent that Lawrence's development as a storyteller conforms to a pattern typical of best traditional storytellers: they are steeped in traditions at home from early childhood, they hear and take an interest in further stories in their environment while they grow up, they begin to tell stories publicly at the age of 40 or 50, whereupon they soon emerge as accomplished storytellers, eagerly adding to their repertoire from whatever sources they come across.

It is, however, only in relation to recently learnt stories that Lawrence had to resort to his amazing ability to remember tales after hearing them only once or twice. The stories he learned in childhood and early youth he heard over and over again. We must not imagine, however, that these stories were stable and unchangeable, repeated more or less word for word. On the contrary we know, thanks to information provided by Lawrence himself, that one and the same story could appear in considerably different forms in his father's telling. An example of this is offered by the story *Goita Skerry*, the two episodes of which Tom sometimes told as separate stories. Indeed, such and other variations were so common as to be the rule rather than the exception.

The storytelling tradition in north Yell was also still, in the first half of the twentieth century, so rich that Lawrence often had the opportunity to hear one and the same tale from more than one teller. This was the case of, for instance, the mysterious legend *The Selkie Boy of Breckon*, which Lawrence heard from his father as well as from another good storyteller, Andrew Williamson of the Brake, Cullivoe. Still other stories were so well known in Lawrence's locality that he might have heard them often from as many as half a dozen storytellers. This – again according to Lawrence's own statement – was the case of the lying tale *The Woolly Horse* which he was first told by the late John Thomas Anderson and later by many others (including his father, as we know thanks to Alan Bruford), and the mysterious folk legend *The Man Who Drowned in Greth*. Certain tales in particular local legends, Lawrence informs us, were even told piece-meal by a group of people, all individuals eager to contribute the specific episodes and details they knew.

It is, to a great extent, as a result of having heard the stories so often and in so many forms that Lawrence has been enabled to make the tales his own property, preserving their main structure and plot with great fidelity but at the same time selecting the best details in description, dialogue and phrase to suit the specific telling occasions and the types of audiences he addresses.

In Lawrence's childhood in north Yell, as no doubt elsewhere in Shetland, there was little or no formality about storytelling. The stories were part and parcel of everyday life, often told during, or in intervals between, ordinary occupations. A valuable example of this is afforded by the note to the story *The Backstone*, which Lawrence heard his father tell 'to the late Bertie Henderson of West-A-Firth in February 1955, when the two of them were clearing snow from the road to Gloup'.

When Lawrence started his storytelling career, on the other hand, he was often addressing larger groups of people, whether in schools or at conferences and festivals. Many of the customs, trades, tools etc. referred to in the old stories would then, as a matter of course, be unknown to the listeners. This would necessitate a

# Introduction
~ ~ ~

greater amount of description and more explanations than storytellers of the old days would ordinarily have been obliged to provide. It is noteworthy how skilfully Lawrence has managed to fill this new need without detriment to the narrative.

In this book Lawrence has wished to introduce his stories to as wide a circle of readers as possible. This has meant that he has been compelled to refrain from presenting them in the dialect in which they were told to him, and in which he would naturally tell them. This has not prevented him, however, from colouring his English with a rich sprinkling of Shetland words and phrases. Readers who want to familiarise themselves with Lawrence's stories in genuine Shetland speech are referred to cassette recordings issued under the titles *For Sic A Hearing, Yul, Hallamas and the Dead of Winter* and *The Backstone*, the first-mentioned of which is also accompanied by a booklet containing a transcription of the original speech.

If I were asked to pick one single story as my favourite from those included in this book, I would probably choose *Jan Tait and the Bear*. My choice is determined not only by reasons already hinted at, but also by the vivid picture it gives of life in ancient Shetland and heroic adventures in Norway. It would hardly be possible to find in oral tradition anything so close to the *thættir*, the short Icelandic tales from the 13th and 14th centuries.

I also share Lawrence's own predilection for the folk legend *The Man Who Drowned in Greth*, dealing with the impossibility of avoiding the manner of death that is in store. This little pearl of eerie fatalism, better known to folklorists under the title *The Hour has Come but not the Man*, is particularly common in Norway and elsewhere in Scandinavia, but it is also found in Scotland. It had a special appeal to Walter Scott who refers to it in the fourth chapter of his novel *The Heart of Midlothian*. Lawrence's version is unusual in that the man destined to drown is a fisherman, who is prevented by his wife through a clever trick from going out to sea. That the drowning occurs in a tub of urine (standing outside many houses in Shetland for the collecting of the fluid necessary in waulking the homemade tweed) is another trait which, as far as I know, is unique.

The tale *Da Slokkit Koli* is also particularly impressive. It contains a variation of the gruesome belief expressed in the proverb

# The Foy and other folk tales
~ ~ ~

'The sea must have its own'. For this reason it was commonly thought to be of no avail to save a drowning man, since even if you were successful it would only mean that you yourself or somebody else would, before long, be certain to be the victim of the enraged sea. In *Da Slokkit Koli*, however, the sea's specific claim to the drowned is reflected in the custom that corpses of sea-drowned people were denied burial in consecrated ground, and interred on the shore, close to the power that claimed them.

Other stories among my favourites are *The Backstone* and *Da Oo Tiggers*. *The Backstone* is about fishing luck, a central concept in the Shetland community in former times; *Da Oo Tiggers* deals with the power of slighted beggar women and the special form of magic they could exercise in causing storms and sinking ships by floating cockle shells and stirring up the water. This is a traditional legend type, *The Ship-sinking Witch,* which is found also in Scotland, Ireland, the Faroes and Iceland. However, again Lawrence's story includes some particular traits, which, as far as I know, are not found elsewhere except in his father's version. These include the women's begging for wool, the dissatisfaction of one of them aroused by being offered black wool instead of white, and the evil witch's failure in the attempt to avenge herself due to the timely interference of the grateful beggar woman who had received white wool.

I would also include *The Selkie Boy of Breckon* and *Goita Skerry* among the stories for which I have a special fondness. *The Selkie Boy of Breckon* is a legend built up around a core of belief in the possibility of conjugal relations between seals and humans, a theme we meet with in numerous stories in the North Sea area. *The Selkie Boy of Breckon* also, in an interesting way, mirrors the prejudices against unmarried mothers in the old Shetland society. *Goita Skerry*, in which the action takes place both in Shetland and Norway, is also a seal story, but this time we are dealing with the age-old belief in shapeshifting, the ability of sorcerers to transform themselves into animals, so prominent in Old Norse as well as later West-Nordic tradition.

The stories referred to so far are typical Shetland tales at the same time as they mirror the Norse heritage of the Islands. This is reflected also in many words and phrases occurring in these tales.

# Introduction
~ ~ ~

That a *bismar* is an old-fashioned instrument for weighing is something Scandinavians of my generation would not be ignorant of – my mother had one in the kitchen (on which I am reputed to have been weighed as a new-born baby swaddled in a cloth). Among other words common to Shetland speech and Scandinavian languages in the tales I have picked are *slokkit,* corresponding to Norwegian *slukket* 'extinguished', *koli,* a lamp of the type the Faroese and the Icelanders call *kola,* and *tigger* 'beggar' which is Norwegian and Danish *tigger,* Swedish *tiggare.*

Specific Shetland qualities, however, may be equally prominent in tales dealing with local history, e.g. those about landlords, ship wrecks, and adventures at sea, Among these are *Heatherdale, The Sheep Thief of Easterhouse, Mees Kees, Life on the Springbank, Robbie's Voyage,* and *Canvas Jackets.* For some of these tales the term 'local' may appear to be a misnomer, considering that Robbie's voyage, in the tale by the same title, took him to Valparaiso, and that the *Springbank* sought harbour in Santa Rosalia in South California. Such sailing trips over the oceans were, however, in recent centuries just as much part and parcel of Shetland life as the connections over the North Sea to Norway in earlier days. The sea stands out as something overwhelmingly important in Shetland life – nobody lived more than a few miles from it – and what is a key concept in life is also a key concept in folklore.

In the event that tales of the categories already referred to should be found too sinister to some readers, there is much else that they can turn to. Take for instance the splendid jocular tales, *The Minister and the Cow, The Woolly Horse* and *The Polar Bear.* These are traditional stories, by no means exclusive to Shetland but, like all the other tales, bestowed with a special Shetland flavour by colourful local details in description and dialogue. *The Polar Bear,* for instance, a story I heard in Sweden, where it was set in Lapland and told about a brown bear, is, in Lawrence's story, placed in Greenland during the times of the whaling industry in the Arctic in which sailors from Shetland were involved. If humour is sought it is also to be found in rich abundance in some of the yarns of Lawrence's own invention mentioned above.

# The Foy and other folk tales
~ ~ ~

Most of the tales in this collection are likely to have their greatest appeal either to grown up readers or to them and youngsters in common. A couple of stories, the fairy tales, *Essypattle and the Blue Yow* and *Da Boy and Da Brunnie,* however, are especially likely to appeal to smaller children. These stories are Shetland versions of wonder tales with counterparts in practically all countries from Ireland to India. Nevertheless, Essypattle is a Shetland Cinderella: her father is a sailor and the fairy god mother a blue ewe. In a similar manner the cake that plays such an important part in *Da Boy and Da Brunnie* is specified as a *brunnie*, a big round Shetland oat-meal cake. By such and other small touches even the most international tales become part of the indigenous tradition. From a scholarly point of view Lawrence's wonder tales are of special interest also for the reason that tales of this kind have only rarely been recorded in the Northern Isles; perhaps they were always rare there.

It would be possible to go on at great length in this way analysing and commenting upon the different kinds of stories. However, I find myself very much in the same situation as a teacher of mine, Åke Campbell of Uppsala in Sweden, who was a renowned folk-life scholar, known among other things for his learned books on traditional bread. Once confronted with a particularly delicious home-made loaf, he is reported to have exclaimed: "I will not study this bread I will eat it!"

In this book everybody, whether Shetlander or non-Shetlander, is offered not only excellent *brunnies* but a full feast, a joyful and splendid *foy*. Everything to tickle the palate and nourish and invigorate body and soul is on the table. I am delighted to have been given the honour to extend the invitation to the treat.

*Bo Almqvist*
*Professor emeritus of Irish Folklore,*
*University College Dublin*

# 1

## Da Boy an Da Brunnie

ONCE upon a time there was a young boy who lived with his mother. One day when he came in to the kitchen she was baking brunnies over a hot fire. Brunnies are the big, round oatcakes made with fat, very much part of the Shetland diet in days gone past.

"I have a job for you," said the mother to her son. "I want you to go to the hill and kann da kye."

By this she meant that she wanted him to check that the cattle were all right and to make sure that they had good grazing. This was necessary because, in the wintertime cattle longed for the warm byre, and they had a habit of returning to the hill dykes, the fencing that separated the hill from the town lands.

The boy willingly agreed to go and, as a reward, his mother gave him a big, thick brunnie to eat on his way. The boy put the brunnie in his pocket, saving it to eat later as a treat. At the hill he found the cattle and did exactly as his mother told him. He then climbed to the top of the Earne's knowe to sit down and eat his brunnie.

As he took the brunnie from his pocket he dropped it. It landed on its edge and rolled all the way down to the bottom of the knowe. The boy thought this good fun so, after fetching it back up to the top, he rolled it down again. This time it did not go all the way to the bottom but disappeared into a thick clump of heather.

Not wanting to lose his brunnie he parted the heather with his hands to look for it. It was then that he discovered a hole in the hill.

At first he thought it to be a rabbit hole but it was so big that he put his head in. In fact, it was so big that he could squeeze his whole body in. He was amazed at what he saw.

He was in a huge cave. It seemed that the whole hill was hollow and there was enough light that he could see. At a distance away from him there was a big fire, and a very big, old woman stirring in a cooking pot that hung above it. Instinctively the boy knew that the old woman was blind so he concentrated on making no sound.

After watching for a time the boy got to thinking that there must be someone else living with the old woman. An old blind woman could not be living all by herself, he reasoned. Therefore, it would be wise to hide in case this 'someone else' came in and discovered him. He could be in big trouble.

Just in time he found a hiding place. He heard heavy footsteps and a lot of commotion. Into the cave, through another entrance, came a giant; a huge, ugly man carrying a bag that he threw into a corner. The bag was full of booty because the giant had been out hunting and looting.

The giant sat down at the table and the old woman dished up, in a huge wooden bowl, the food from the cooking pot. The giant ate, and ate, a giant meal before sitting back in his chair with a contented look on his face. But not for long. He raised his big, ugly, hairy face and began to sniff the air.

Sitting upright, he roared in a terrible voice, "Fee fy foe fum, I smell the blood of an Earthly man, be he living or be he dead, I'll have his head with my supper bread!"

So saying, he got up and began to search the cave. It took him hardly any time at all to home in on the boy. Reaching in, he hauled the boy out of his hiding place and held him up to take a close look at him.

"This is no use for eating," declared the giant, in a pained voice. "This boy is far too small to eat, there is no flesh on him and he would only be one mouthful for a hungry giant."

After some thought, he ordered the old woman to tether the boy by his little finger to the stoop of the mill, and feed him every day with meal and milk.

"When the boy's leg, at the thickest part, is as thick as my little finger, then he will be ready for eating," the giant added.

Every night, when the giant came home from his day's hunting and looting, he would examine the boy. At last the night came when the giant declared that the boy was big enough and he ordered the old woman to boil him for the next day's dinner.

They spoke quietly about it. They did not want the boy to know because he might put up a struggle. The next morning the old woman put on a bigger fire than usual, and above it she hung the biggest pot, two thirds full of water.

When the water was hot she came to the boy and said, in her sweetest voice, "I need your help. I want you to climb up on my back and tell me if the water is boiling."

The boy was alert to what was planned for him and he knew that if he agreed the old woman would tip him into the boiling water.

"I am just a stupid boy," he said, "I know nothing about cooking and I don't know if water is boiling or not. We will do it the other way round. If you go on my back you will be close to the pot and, even if you are blind, you will know if the water is boiling."

To humour him the old woman agreed. She was awful heavy for the boy to lift but he was desperate. He managed to get to his feet, dump the old woman into the kettle and put on the lid. He put more peats on the fire and from time to time he checked the water level, but he boiled the old woman all day. He figured that, because she was old, she would take a lot of cooking.

In the evening, before the giant came home, the boy dredged the old woman from the cooking pot and served her up on the table for the giant. He then found five round pebbles, put them in his pocket, and climbed on a ledge that was directly above the giant's dining table. He did not have long to wait before the giant came in as hungry as a hunter. He sat down and began to devour the old woman.

As the boy suspected she was not very tender. "Tough, tough," the giant said over and over, but he kept on eating.

When he could eat no more he sat back and fell fast asleep, his mouth fell open and he snored loudly. The boy took careful aim and dropped the round pebbles, one by one, into the giant's mouth. The giant gulped and choked, the stones stuck fast in his gullet and they killed him.

When the boy was sure the giant could do him no more harm he came down from the roof of the cave. For the first time he was able to have a proper look at the cave. He found the place where the giant kept all his treasure, so filled up a bag with as much as he could carry.

He was glad to leave the cave and go home to his mother. With the giant's treasure they were able to live in peace, and with plenty, for all the days of their lives.

*I have known this story all my life. I do not remember learning it but I heard it from my father.*

# 2

## Essypattle and the Blue Yow

ONCE upon a time there was a man and his wife who lived in a lovely little cottage by the sea. They had one daughter and they loved her very much. She was always helping her mother in the kitchen and she was always willing to do whatever her parents asked her to do. She was the apple of her father's eye, he adored her and whenever he was home he spoilt her.

However, he was not home that often. He was a seaman and he had to go away to sail. Sometimes he was away for lengthy periods and he would long to get home again to see his family. They were all so happy together and the little girl loved the times when her father was home.

One time when he was home tragedy struck the family. The mother took ill and died. The girl and her father were heartbroken. They were left by themselves and they had to learn to live without the one they both loved so much. As there was no one to look after the girl her father could not go back to sea and he had to stay home with her.

After a time they ran short of money. The man knew no other trade but sailoring so back to sea he had to go. He had to get someone to look after his daughter and the only way he could do that was to remarry. He proposed to a woman who lived in the next village. She was a widow and she had two daughters, older girls. All of them promised to be kind and good to the sailor's daughter.

When he went away the stepmother and the stepsisters were not long in breaking their promise. They made the girl do all the hard work. She had to clean out the fireplace, fetch peats for the fire and wash and scrub the kitchen and the floors. She was so unhappy. No matter how hard she worked, or how hard she tried, they were always scolding and shouting at her.

Although she had to cook for all of them she seldom got anything nice to eat, she was given scraps and leftovers. When her father sent money the stepmother and her daughters kept it all to themselves. They used it to buy nice clothes while the girl only had rags to wear. She knew that it would be a long, long time before her father came home again, and sometimes at night she cried herself to sleep.

When she had time to herself, and this was seldom, she used to spread out the ashes on the hearth and draw pictures in them. Her cruel stepsisters called her Essypattle, a nickname that was to stay with her for a long time. Essypattle did have two friends; one of them a crow and the other the blue yow. The blue yow was an unusual coloured sheep. It was grey but when the fleece was opened up a pale blue shade was discernable. This is rare but not unknown in Shetland.

The crow would come and peck at the window and no matter how hungry Essypattle was, or how little she had for herself, she always found a few crumbs to give to her friend. Every day she would go outside and speak to the blue yow and pat her kindly on the head.

One day the stepsisters came home in a state of high excitement. They had heard the sensational news that the king was coming to their village to pay a visit. They began to consider, and argue, about what they would wear on the big day.

Of course, there was no question of Essypattle going to see the king, because she had no clothes other than the rags she wore every day when she did all the dirty work. Neither her stepmother nor her stepsisters would give her anything else to wear so she just sat home and drew pictures in the ashes with the tears rolling down her cheeks.

# Essypattle and the Blue Yow

~ ~ ~

The crow came pecking at the window. She got up to look for something to give him. The crow was trying to tell her something. "Go to the blue yow, go to the blue yow," he kept saying, over and over again.

Thinking that the blue yow needed her help in some way, she hurried outside. When she got to the blue yow she was suddenly aware of a change coming over her. When she looked down at herself she found that she was wearing a beautiful silk, snow white dress. It was the most beautiful dress she had ever seen, far better than any of the dresses owned by her stepsisters.

After she got over the shock of this magic, her first thought was that if her stepsisters saw this lovely dress they would not allow her to keep it, they would steal it from her and keep it for themselves. She thoughtfully made her way back home. She went into her bedroom and took off the magic dress and hid it away, then put on some of the old ragged clothes that she was more used to wearing

When the other three came back from seeing the king they were talking, non-stop, about the royal visit and what the king had said. The king's son, the crown prince, was looking for a bride, a young lady to become a princess and some day, the queen. The king had declared that he was going to send his most trusted servant to look for a suitable girl. He would have with him a pair of slippers. Any girl whose feet could fit the slippers would be the princess.

The sisters were determined that one of them would become the princess and eagerly waited the day when the king's servant was due to bring the slippers. In the fullness of time the big day arrived and every girl in the village wanted to try on the slippers. As always, Essypattle stayed at home with the ashes, the crow and the blue yow for company.

When they saw the slippers the sisters were totally dismayed. It was abundantly clear that to fit their big ugly feet into the slippers was out of the question. One of them gave up immediately but the other, her heart so set on being the princess, was prepared to take desperate measures. With a grim look on her face she went home and into the barn behind the cottage.

She picked up the sharpest axe and put first one bare foot, then the other, on the chopping block and cut off her toes. Ignoring the pain, and the blood, she went back, demanded the slippers, and put them on. With her toes missing the slippers fitted, and the king's man had to admit that she might have the right to become the princess. Whatever misgivings he may have had, his instructions were to find a girl who could wear the slippers. This he had done.

He took the girl up in front of him on the saddle of his horse and set off back to the palace. As they galloped along, Essypattle's friend, the crow, hovered above them reciting a rhyme:

> *"Nippit fit an clippit fit*
> *Ower da meadow rides,*
> *While blyde fit an boannie fit,*
> *In the hus bides."*

The king's man asked what the crow had said but her feet were so painful that she was crying and didn't answer. When they arrived at the palace they were met by the king, but the girl who was wearing the slippers in no way impressed him.

"Where did you find this lass?" he asked. "She might be a nice enough person," he added, "but she is no princess."

The servant explained that she was the only girl he could find who could wear the slippers. As he looked at the girl he knew that the king was right. The girl was no beauty at the best of times, but with her face distorted by pain and tear-stained she was far from attractive.

The king took the slippers from her feet and when he saw what she had done, he was horrified. The king was a kindly man and he felt sorry for her. He said to his servant, "Take this poor silly lass back to where you found her."

And to the girl he said, "You have been very stupid, you have mutilated your feet for nothing, you are not a princess and you never will be."

Again the king's man took her up on his horse and as they neared the cottage again the crow was overhead. This time his rhyme was:

> *"Nippit fit is coarse an pert*
> *While blyde fit sits by the hert."*

# Essypattle and the Blue Yow

~ ~ ~

Again the king's servant did not understand and again the girl was unable to tell him. The sister hobbled into the cottage and when Essypattle saw the state of her feet she, too, felt sorry for her. Despite all the nasty things that her stepsister had done to her, Essypattle took a bowl of warm water and a soft cloth, bathed her stepsister's feet, bandaged them and made them as comfortable as possible.

All this time the king's servant looked on. He could see that underneath all the dirt and the rags Essypattle was a really beautiful girl, maybe beautiful enough to be a princess.

"Do you have nothing better to wear?" he asked.

"Oh yes," replied Essypattle, "I have the dress that I got from the blue yow."

She hurriedly washed her face and ran to her bedroom and put on the silk dress. The king's servant now saw her as the loveliest young lady in the whole world. When she was given the all important slippers to try they fitted her feet perfectly. The king's man lost no time in taking Essypattle to the palace.

Everyone at the palace was enchanted by Essypattle's beauty and charm. The crown prince fell madly in love with her and she with him, and the king arranged the royal wedding as soon as possible. And so it was that Essypattle, the prince, the crow and the blue yow lived happily ever after.

*This version of the Cinderella story is well known in Shetland but I heard this from my father.*

# 3

## Da Oo Tiggers

LONG ago in Shetland, some unwelcome visitors went from door to door begging for wool. Housewives felt obliged to be nice to them because the oo tiggers had an evil reputation as witches. Bad things happened to anyone who did not give them wool and show kindness.

Two oo tiggers, women, came to a house in the north of the island of Yell. In this house lived two sisters, their husbands and families. At the time only the sisters were at home; the men were at the fishing and the children were at school. The oo tiggers were invited in and one of the sisters put on the kettle to make tea. The other sister went to see what she could find in the way of wool.

It was early summer so wool was scarce. All the wool from the previous year had been spun into yarn and knitted during the long, dark Shetland winter. Nonetheless, she did find a little and one oo tigger was given some white wool, while the other got some black.

The one with the white wool was well satisfied but the other, with the black wool, was not at all pleased. She didn't drink her tea. She set down the cup with a crash and stormed out of the house. Unconcerned at first, the other sipped her tea and chatted to the sisters. Then she too became alarmed and ran outside, shouting, "There is evil in the air."

The sisters followed after. The oo tigger ran up the yard, through a gap in the stone wall and down into the valley, where the Burn of Midbrake runs serenely through the meadows.

10

# Da Oo Tiggers

~ ~ ~

When they got close enough they saw the oo tigger, the one who was given the black oo, crouching at the edge of a wide, still pool. She was bowing and chanting. She had three cockleshells floating in the water and she was throwing in small stones to make ripples. The shells were bobbing up and down, water had splashed into them and they were barely afloat.

The second oo tigger shouted at her to stop throwing stones and shoved her, roughly, out of the way. She then, very carefully, lifted the three shells, one by one, out of the burn, setting them on the bank, side by side. After that the two oo tiggers went on their way and the two sisters went back home.

The men came home early from the fishing that day with no fish. They had had a nasty experience and they could not understand what had happened. The weather was good, no wind and smooth seas. All of a sudden the sea got very rough; mountainous seas that threatened to swamp the boats.

The three boats belonged to the Laird of Midbrake and in each of the boats there was a man from the house that was visited by the oo tiggers. The men told of how quickly the sea got up. They believed that their end had come, water came aboard the boat in such quantity that even baling as hard as they could they had little chance of staying afloat.

Then, as quickly as the storm arose, it died away again and the sea went back to being as smooth as it was at the start. Not even the oldest of the fishermen could ever remember anything like this happening before.

But the women knew what had happened because the sudden storm at sea happened at exactly the same time as the oo tigger was working her black magic with the cockleshells in the burn.

*I heard my father tell this story many times.*

11

# 4

# London Again

ONCE, when a fishing boat was working offshore, it was caught in a sudden storm. It was an open boat, a sixtreen, with six men on board. The wind had come without warning but it blew them towards the shore and their home beach. They knew that they would get to the beach but the big problem was in making a safe landing.

As it happened, matters were taken out of the fishermen's control. The boat was lifted on to the crest of a huge wave and propelled forward at breakneck pace. The sea carried them ashore and on to the crown of the beach where they landed with a resounding crash, but with all the men still on board.

The men found, to their relief, that none of them was seriously hurt, there were no broken bones but they all had cuts and bruises. When they inspected the boat they found a different story, it was badly damaged and it would need major repairs before it was seaworthy again. The worst of the damage was to the keel; it was broken and would have to be replaced.

Each man made his way home in a thoughtful frame of mind. On the one hand they were thankful there were no serious injuries but, on the other hand, the loss of the boat for weeks on end meant they would have no income, and to poor people it was going to make life even harder.

When the skipper of the sixtreen arrived home he found that his wife had her own problems. She met him on the green and

# London Again

~ ~ ~

demanded that he find a new piece of rope for a standing baand to the cow. The standing baand is a short tedder, tied in a loop around a cow's horns to keep her in her own stall in the byre.

The skipper paid little heed to her demands. He was far more worried about the boat and the finding of a suitable piece of wood for a new keel. The following morning at daybreak he set out to walk to see a boat builder with a view to obtaining a suitable plank of wood. It was a long, long way and he was very disappointed to find that the boat builder could not help him.

However, he was told of another man who repaired boats, so he walked on there in his quest to have his precious boat fixed. Unfortunately, this man had no wood available either, and by this time it was night. The skipper was offered food and a bed for the night which he gladly accepted. Next morning he set off again, doggedly determined to find the wood that he needed.

He was now very far away from home and in places that he did not know. There were long, bleak stretches of empty road with no houses or signs of life. The skipper walked on and on and by the middle of the afternoon he was tired, cold and hungry. The weather was closing in, it was windy and it began to rain. His priority now was to find food and shelter.

After dark, when he was almost despairing, he saw a faint light in the distance ahead. He quickened his step and came to the house that was showing the light and he knocked on the door. A middle-aged woman answered. He asked if he could stay the night but she offered him no welcome and no hospitality.

He asked if there were any other houses near and she said no, they had no neighbours. He pleaded his case and the woman very reluctantly allowed him in to the house. Inside were two other women, one about the same age as the one who answered the door and another, much older, perhaps the mother.

They gave him some stale bread and a cup of milk, As soon as he was finished it one of them showed him into a bedroom. He found this very odd because it was still early evening and not a time when an adult would consider retiring for the night.

When he looked around the room he found that it was sparsely furnished indeed. There was a bed but the only other item of furniture was a large chest. He lay on the bed but did not undress, in truth he was tired and it was quite pleasant to relax, although he was somewhat uneasy. He did not like the three women, he did not trust them, and they had a certain air of evil about them.

After some considerable length of time he was aware of the bedroom door slowly opening. He pretended to be asleep but he watched through one half-open eye. It was one of the younger women. She didn't even glance at him but went straight to the chest and opened the lid. She took out a hat – a beret – and put it on her head.

"London again!" she said, in a loud voice.

To the skipper's astonishment she vanished. One moment she was there and the next instant she had completely disappeared. The first thought that came to his mind was that he had been sleeping without realising it and this was something he had dreamed.

When another of the women came into the room he was wide awake but, again, he pretended to be asleep. He need not have worried. The woman was totally focused on the chest. She lifted the lid, took out a beret, put it on her head and said the magic words, "London again," and, just like the other woman, she was gone in an instant.

The man had seen this clearly but he refused to believe his eyes, he wondered if he had lost his sanity. Almost immediately the third woman appeared in the bedroom and the process was repeated.

# London Again
~ ~ ~

So troubled was he that there was no question of sleep. After a time, he got up and left the bedroom. He made his way to the kitchen fully expecting to find the women there and he had decided that he would pretend to be thirsty and ask for a drink of water. The kitchen was empty but the fire was burning bright. He called out but got no answer. He explored the whole house until he was satisfied that he was the only person in it.

Going back to the kitchen he looked through the cupboards and made himself a meal of bread and cheese and boiled water to make a pot of tea. He sat by the fire until he felt relaxed and then decided to go back to bed again. He was still tired from all the walking of the last two days and he felt ready to sleep.

In the bedroom curiosity got the better of him and he was drawn towards the chest. When he looked inside he saw dozens of berets; he took one out and put it on his head and said, "London again." He, too, took off. He experienced the sensation of going through the air at the speed of light and within the blink of an eye he landed again.

Looking around, he saw he was in a strange place but the women were there. They were all lying on the floor sleeping, with a cup near each of them. He was in a wine cellar. There were dozens of hogsheads stacked around the walls and a few barrels laid up on trestles, with spigots in them.

He filled a cup with wine and drank it. It was the most delicious wine he had ever tasted so he had another, and another, and another. The next thing he knew he was surrounded by several men and one of them was speaking in a loud, angry voice. He was clearly the owner of the wine cellar and the rest were policemen, but there were no signs of the women.

The vintner was telling the policemen how a thief had, for years, been stealing wine from him. Pointing at the skipper, he announced triumphantly that he had caught him at last. The skipper protested and tried to tell his side of the story but no one listened. The policemen dragged him away and threw him into jail.

He was charged with theft and was put on trial. Again he pleaded and begged someone to believe his story, but he was found guilty. In those days in London, convicted thieves were put to death, and the judge ordered that the skipper be hanged by the neck until he was dead. A date was fixed for his execution and he was put into a condemned cell to await the fatal day.

When that day came he was taken by horse-drawn cart to the scaffold. Hangings were open to the public and a large crowd of people had assembled to watch him die. He was a brave man and he was defiant as he climbed the steps. Before putting the noose around his neck the hangman, in time-honoured fashion, asked if he had any last request.

It came to him like a bolt out of the blue. He still had the magic beret in his pocket so he asked the hangman for permission to wear his own hat when he died. This request was readily granted and, putting the hat on his head, he said, "Home again." The skipper, the scaffold and the hangman took off like a rocket and, as they did so, the skipper kicked the hangman over the edge.

In an instant he landed at the gable of his own house. He had been away for so long that the folks at home had become worried about him and some of the sixtreen's crew, at that moment, were visiting his wife to ask if there was any news of him.

When the men saw the scaffold they could not contain their excitement. "That wood," they exclaimed, "is perfect for the keel of the boat."

Seizing the hangman's rope with the noose on the end, his wife said, "And this rope is just the job for a new standing baand for the cow!"

*My grandmother had this story but it is so long ago that I have only the faintest recollection of her telling it. I have heard many versions of it since.*

# 5

## Robbie Anderson

ROBBIE Anderson lived in Cullivoe, Yell, with his wife and three children. Like all their friends and neighbours the Andersons were poor people. They eked out a living from the land, the fishing and some spinning and knitting. One thing, however, marked out Robbie Anderson from all the other men – he was a brilliant fiddle player.

He was, by common consent, far and away the best fiddler in the parish. But many, hearing Robbie play for the first time, declared that he was the best they had ever heard. He was the first to be invited to any wedding, foy, or gathering of any kind.

One Owld Yul Een when Robbie was walking along a path on his way to feed animals he was accosted by a tiny little man with red hair. Robbie knew at once that this man was a trow. He was not very pleased to see him; Robbie preferred to have nothing to do with either trows or any supernatural beings. Any mortal who offended the trows could find themselves in a lot of trouble.

This trow spoke to Robbie in a quiet, pleasant voice. "Robbie," he said, "I want you to come and play at our Owld Yul Foy."

"I'm sorry," Robbie replied, "this I cannot do. On Owld Yul Een I go with my family to visit friends. We play and dance and drink and sing. On any other night of the year I would consider it but not on Owld Yul Een."

The trow said, "So, so, Robbie, I hear what you say and I take no offence but if you change your mind I will make it very worth your

while. If you do come to play for us you must not tell anyone where you have gone or been; not your wife, not your children, not your friends, no one at all."

With that the trow disappeared leaving Robbie in a thoughtful frame of mind. They had no money and to be paid for playing a fiddle was something that Robbie never believed possible, not even in his wildest dreams. Not to be able to tell his wife or discuss it with anyone was a serious drawback but he knew that, in this regard, the trow must be obeyed. To get on the wrong side of the trows was living very dangerously.

Robbie found his decision really hard to make but when night came he took his fiddle under his arm and set off towards the trowie hadd. When he got there a door in the hillside was open, light streamed out and there were sounds of laughter, the clinking of glasses and much talking. The same trow who had invited Robbie was there to meet him.

He led Robbie in and showed him a long table laden with food and drink. The trow told Robbie to help himself, to eat and drink as much as he wanted. He also showed Robbie a corner, near the table, where he could stand and play his fiddle. As Robbie looked around he saw scores of trows; men, women and children, all there, it seemed, to enjoy the foy.

The buffet table had on it the most delicious food that Robbie had ever seen. They had meat, fruit, cheese, bread and many things well beyond Robbie's experience. As for the drinks, he knew not what any of them were. Much as he was tempted Robbie avoided eating or drinking anything at all. He did not trust the trows. He had heard stories of men who had taken trowie liquor. They thought they had been away for a few minutes but it could be a hundred years before they came back to the human world.

The trows loved Robbie's music. They danced, reeled, whirled, stepped and hooched hour after hour. As for Robbie, he played like a man inspired. Spring after spring flowed effortlessly from his fiddle and he found himself playing tunes that he had never heard before. He played until it was morning and the daylight was appearing in the morning sky.

By this time even the trows were tired. Robbie noticed that only a few were still dancing and all the children had disappeared. Eventually Robbie was left on his own. He was exhausted, so he made his weary way home, a deeply unhappy man. The trow had promised pay but he had given Robbie nothing, not even a thank you. He did not even say goodbye.

He dreaded the reunion with his wife. He shuddered to think what she might believe of him. He had refused to tell her where he was going and now he could not tell where he had been. He was right, she did give him a very frosty reception, she demanded an explanation and she accused him of being with another woman. All this he endured. He did not say one word in his own defence.

The next week or so was a bad time for the Andersons, they seldom spoke to each other and the tension affected the children. However, as time went on and January drew to a close, things slowly returned to something like normal. The last day of January brought a severe blizzard. It was one of the biggest snowfalls in living memory; the snow was many feet deep.

When the snow stopped falling, the sky cleared, the wind fell and the frost was severe. Day after day was clear, calm and with bright sunshine. The sea lay without a ripple, like a mirror. Some of Robbie's neighbours suggested they try some fishing. Robbie readily agreed, opportunities to fish in mid-winter came but seldom and a feed of fresh fish would be a welcome change from the salt food that was the usual winter diet.

When they got to the grounds none of them had ever seen fish so plentiful or so easy to catch. The moment that a fly was put in the water it filled with fish. In an incredible, hectic hour of fishing the boat was full to the gunwales and to take more would make the boat unsafe. It was prime fish too, it was the spawning time and every fish was fat and round with roe.

Not only did they have plenty of fish for themselves but they were able to give fish freely to all their friends and neighbours. The next day dawned bright and fair so the men went back to the fishing at first light. It was the same as the day before; the fish seemed to be fighting to get into the boat. Every day after that was a repeat and soon every house in the parish had fish and fish salted.

One day when Robbie's friends suggested yet another fishing trip, Robbie declined. "I have a lot of work to do at home," he said. "I need to take oats and hay into the barn for the animals and I would need to dig out a path to the well. Perhaps we will go some other day, if the fine weather holds."

The other men went to the fishing without Robbie but this time they caught very little, just enough to be a meal for each of them. Nobody was surprised. The fishing, as it had been, was too good to be true. Two days later they went off to the sea again and this time Robbie went too. The fishing was the same as at first, fish galore and so easy to catch; the fish took bare hooks, there was no need for bait.

This set Robbie's brain racing. He began to wonder if the good fishing luck had anything to do with the trows. Was this their way of paying him? He kept those thoughts to himself but he wondered if he would ever find out the truth. In any event the weather changed and fishing was no longer possible. The thaw came with gales and rain from the south-east and the snow gradually disappeared.

The men of the township now had a new priority, to go to the hills and look for the sheep. The snow had lasted for four weeks and nearly all the sheep had been buried beneath the deep snow. They all expected big losses and some of the crofters lost anything up to half of their total stock. Everyone had losses, except Robbie, he had not lost a single animal.

When lambing time came each of Robbie's ewes had twins; strong, healthy lambs, and the mothers had plenty of rich milk for them to thrive on. And so it went on all through the summer. Everything that Robbie did worked well for him; plenty of fish, plenty of lambs and all the crops grew exceptionally well. Although nothing was said, Robbie now knew that his luck could not be natural.

Proof of the trows' involvement, if proof were needed, came in the autumn. The oats and the bere were ripe, golden and ready for harvesting when the gales came. Gales and rain in September are seasonal but this year they were so severe that they destroyed the crops. The grain was all flattened; it lay on the earth, a tangled soggy mass; very little of it could be saved.

Again Robbie's crops were the exception. His corn waved golden in the breeze with not a broken straw. It was the best harvest he had ever had. He had so much winter fodder that he was able to take on another cow. None of Robbie's stock would go hungry during this winter. No doubt folk wondered at Robbie's good fortune but, again, nothing was said or asked.

When Owld Yul Een came around again Robbie made a point of walking along the same path that he was on a year ago. Again the little red-haired trow met him and asked him to play at their foy. This time Robbie didn't hesitate and agreed at once to go to the trowie hadd. Again the trow reminded Robbie that he must not tell anyone and this, too, he promised.

Just as last year Robbie refrained from either eating or drinking but played his fiddle all night, until the trows were all exhausted. This time Robbie's wife was a little less hostile. Maybe she could guess where he had been, maybe she followed him, but in any case the Anderson household did not have the unhappiness of the year before. Robbie's good luck was the same. It seemed that he could do no wrong.

And so it went on, year after year. It was taken for granted that Robbie disappeared every Owld Yul Een and everyone got used to it. Through all the good luck that the trows brought, Robbie and his family were no longer poor people. With the children grown up, they were very comfortable indeed.

However, the year came when the trow failed to appear. As in every previous year Robbie walked along the same path. He thought that, perhaps, he had got the time wrong. He went again, but no trow. He spent the entire day walking up and down but without success. Robbie was very undecided about what to do, but when night came he took his fiddle as usual and set out for the trowie hadd. It had become a habit. It was expected of him.

When he got there he knew at once that things were not the way they used to be. The place was as silent as the grave. There were no voices, no clinking of glasses, no singing and no laughter. He was about to turn away when he saw, in the furthest corner, a tiny light. As he ventured nearer he could see a very small fire, just two or three peats burning in a red glow. Beside the fire sat an old woman. She knew who Robbie was; she was there the first night Robbie had played for the trows.

She looked up. "Thanks for coming, Robbie," she said, "but you are not needed here any more."

"Where is everyone?" asked Robbie. "Is there no Owld Yul Foy this year?"

"Everybody has left here," she told Robbie. "I am the only one left. You see, there is a new minister in the place. He hates us trows and he preaches vehemently against us, so much so that my folk cannot abide it. They have all gone to the Faroe Islands to be away from him, but for my part, I am too old to move, and besides, I am kinda deaf and I cannot hear him."

Slowly, reluctantly, Robbie made his way home. They were all surprised to see him but they celebrated Owld Yul Een as they used to do, many years ago. Ever after that Robbie had no more trowie luck. He was an ordinary man again. Some things went well for him and other things did not work for him at all.

*This was one of my father's favourite stories.*

# 6

# The Skull

IN BYGONE days in Shetland, before a wedding, certain procedures always took place. One of these was the observance of the contract night. This was invariably the Saturday night before the proclamation (the banns) was read out by the minister in church on the Sunday morning.

The bridegroom, along with his best man, would collect the proclamation from the session clerk and deliver it to the manse for the minister's attention. Afterwards, the two would go to the bride's house with the sporing bottle. The sporing bottle would be filled with whisky or other spirits, and symbolically, it sealed the bargain.

The bridegroom would offer his father-in-law-to-be a glass of the spirits. By accepting the drink the bride's father accepted that the groom was a part of the family and a member of the household. By offering the drink the bridegroom pledged himself to go through with the marriage and to accept all the responsibilities that a marriage entailed.

This bridegroom had quite a distance to walk before he got to the house of the best man. After a time he realised that his dog was with him. The dog went everywhere with him but he did not want the dog that night. He ordered the dog to go home but he was young and not always obedient and he just stayed with his master.

Sometimes the dog would run away ahead chasing rabbits and whenever he found something interesting he would lag behind. The bridegroom, after a time ignored him, after all he had more important things on his mind.

When he was opposite the graveyard the bridegroom found the dog playing with a human skull on the road. The dog threw the skull up in the air then tried to catch it when it came down again. When it rolled away along the road the dog chased it. He was having great fun.

The bridegroom took the skull from the dog. He assumed it had come from the graveyard but how it came to be on the road was a total mystery.

As he held the skull in his hands, the bridegroom said to it, "If you had been a living man I would have invited you to my wedding, but because you are just a skull, I will put you in a place where neither my dog, nor any dog, will molest you again."

So saying, he pushed the skull into a rabbit burrow as deep as it would go. He then covered the hole with stones and earth. He went on his way, full of the joys of life, full of excitement about his forthcoming wedding, and he took no time at all to forget about the skull.

The bridegroom and the best man completed their business with the session clerk and the minister and proceeded to the bride's house where they were met with a great welcome. They all drank generously from the sporing bottle, the bride's father had a bottle as well and the women of the house provided a delicious supper of lamb, bannocks, home made bread and cakes. A great night was had by all.

The wedding day came at last and relations, friends and well-wishers packed the kirk. Afterwards, the bridal party and invited guests gathered in the bride's house for the wedding feast and the dancing. The ben end of the house had been cleared to make room for the dancing and the fiddler sat on the churn in the corner and played with the utmost skill and verve.

In those days wedding dances continued all night. No one thought of going home until the daylight appeared. Food and refreshments were passed around the guests at regular intervals and the newly married couple led the Shetland reels.

In the middle of the night a knock came to the door. In Shetland no one locked doors; any visitor simply opened the door and entered. A knock on the door was so unexpected, and such a surprise, that the dancing stopped, the fiddle fell silent, and the whole house came to a standstill.

When the door was opened the visitor standing on the doorstep was clearly a total stranger. He asked to speak to the bridegroom. The bridegroom spoke to the stranger and asked what he wanted.

"I want you to come with me," replied the man, "I will not keep you long."

"I am staying here, I am going nowhere," the bridegroom stated very firmly. "I will not leave my bride or the guests on my wedding night."

So persuasive was the visitor that the bridegroom agreed to go with him for the short time promised. They walked some way from the house and as their eyes became accustomed to the gloom the bridegroom began to feel even more uneasy. He was certain that he knew the village thoroughly, but now he found himself in unfamiliar surroundings.

Never before had he seen either the road they were on or the houses near to it. The stranger led them to a big, well-lit house, on a hillside. The front door was open and the groom was shown into a large, lavishly furnished, drawing room. Such a room the bridegroom had never seen before.

The stranger indicated an armchair beside a hearty fire and told the bridegroom to sit. He sat down but got up again immediately in a state of great alarm. He had glanced up toward the ceiling and there, hanging above the chair by a single hair, was an enormous millstone. It looked as though the massive stone would fall at any second.

The stranger smiled. "Do not be afraid," he said, "I will no more allow the millstone to fall on your head than you would allow your dog to play with my skull!"

Now the bridegroom was really frightened. "What do want from me?" demanded the groom. "I do not want to be here. I want to go back to my wife and the wedding reception."

"All I want from you," he was told, "is a little of your time."

The stranger picked up a candle from the table and he made a mark in the wax with his thumbnail. "When the candle burns down to that mark you are free to go and I will never trouble you again."

No more was said, but the bridegroom never took his eyes from the candle. After what seemed an age the mark finally disappeared and the bridegroom got up and left. The stranger made no move to stop him. Outside, the dawn was near, and the first greek of a new day was to be seen in the sky.

As he retraced his steps the bridegroom was aware that he was returning to a place that he knew. In the early morning light he saw familiar landmarks and houses and, before long, he was outside the house he had left with the stranger. Impatient as he was to get to the wedding party, his step faltered, he instinctively knew that something was very wrong.

There was no sound from the house, no music, no talking, no laughter and no sound of dancers' feet on the floor. He pushed open the door and went in. In the gloom, the near darkness, he could discern the shape of an old woman in the act of lighting a fire and sweeping the hearth.

Puzzled, he went up to her and asked what had become of the wedding company.

"You are in the wrong house," she replied. "There is no wedding here."

"I am not in the wrong house." The bridegroom indicated his wedding suit. "It was my wedding here last night. Where is my bride? Where are the wedding guests? And where is my family?" he asked, imploringly.

The old woman, slowly, painfully, straightened her back. She considered for a time and then said, "There was no wedding here last night, or for many a night before that, but when I was a child I heard my grandmother, she was very old at the time, tell of a wedding in this house where the bridegroom went away with a stranger and he was never seen again."

When the bridegroom heard this the horrible truth dawned on him. He had not been away for a half hour or so. He had been away for several generations. Before the old woman's eyes he changed from a young, handsome bridegroom to an older man, then to a really old man, and finally collapsed into a little pile of dust on the floor.

The old woman had a flat wooden board in her hand that served as a fire shovel – an essy brod. She bent down, swept him up with her brush and threw him into the fire. And that was the finish of him.

*Another of my father's stories. I have known it for as long as I can remember.*

# 7

## Da Slokkit Koli

SHETLAND is a group of islands devoid of trees. Therefore, timber is in short supply and valuable. All through history Shetland men have been ardent beachcombers. Whenever there is an onshore wird men, in number, can be seen going aboot da banks.

Once, long ago, a large quantity of quality wood was driven into the Geo of Funzie and every able bodied man in Fetlar was there to save the wood and take it ashore. No one knew where the wood had come from; it could have been that a ship had lost a deck cargo or maybe it was something worse, a ship may have foundered.

It was a short winter day so the Fetlar men did not stop for any rest or even dinner. They continued to drag as much of the wood as they could ashore. In the afternoon, when the sky was mirkening, they made a grim discovery, a corpse. It was the body of a seaman; that much was evident from the clothes he wore.

The dead man had been clearly aware of his mortal danger because he was, even in death, clutching under his arms, a capstan bar. He had hoped, no doubt, that the wooden bar would give him sufficient buoyancy to keep his head above the water. Whether he had died from the cold or whether he had drowned it was impossible to tell, but most certainly he was dead.

In those days, any dead person washed ashore by the sea was not buried in the graveyard. They were always buried as close to the sea as possible. People believed in the power of the sea Gods. If the sea had claimed a life then it was wrong and dangerous to take that body away from the sea, but a decent burial, nonetheless, was needed.

The Fetlar men found a soft piece of ground near the beach and dug a grave. They did not make a coffin for the dead seaman but they lined the grave with wood. They lined the bottom with short pieces of board and did the same with the sides.

When the corpse was laid to rest they were about to cover it with wood when one man remarked on the boots that the dead man was wearing. The boots were almost new, they had wooden soles but the uppers were made of thick but pliable leather.

"I am going to have those boots," said the man. "I know by looking at them that they are just the right size."

The other men, especially the older ones, were horrified at the very idea. They told him, in no uncertain terms, that he was going to do no such thing. To steal from a dead man was unthinkable. The man who wanted the boots said no more, he seemed to accept that to take them was wrong.

When the interment was complete all the men went home. The finding of the dead man had taken from them their appetite for saving any more wood and, besides, it was nearly pitch dark. Perhaps the wood would still be in the geo tomorrow.

The wind died away in the evening and the nearly full moon shone brightly on a clear lift. One man kept looking out from the door of his house; the man who coveted the boots. Furtively, with a spade, he returned to the grave, opened it and, with great difficulty, pulled the boots from the dead man's feet.

He put the grave back the way it was and made his way back home. He was well aware that if he openly wore the boots the other men would know where they had come from. His plan was to hide the boots in the barn and then, next year perhaps, when everyone had forgotten about the incident, it would be safe to wear them.

A few nights later he was in his barn and about to thresh corn. He had a koli lamp for light but the lamp kept going out. He found this strange as there was no draught and the oil in the lamp was fresh and good quality. Thinking that the wick may be faulty he went into the house and brought back a piece of new linen.

He shaped the linen and soaked it in the oil. When the new wick was lit it burned with a bright, even light. As soon as he restarted work the lamp went out again and this told him that something very strange was happening. He lit the lamp yet again but this time he watched it, determined to find out why it kept going out.

He did not have long to wait. A hand appeared from the doorway. It was a thin, withered, white hand with long, dirty black fingernails. The hand, on a long thin arm, reached out for the lamp and the index finger played with the flame. It was clear that the finger felt no pain and the flame did not burn the flesh. Then, all of a sudden, the forefinger and thumb compressed the wick, snuffing out the flame.

It took all the courage that the Fetlar man could muster to go outside, but he knew that he had to confront this apparition. There was just enough light from the moon and stars to make out the figure of a man leaning against the wall of the barn. There was no mistaking who he was. He was the corpse from the Geo of Funzie.

The Fetlar man was terrified but asked in a shaky voice what the ghost wanted.

"I want my boots," he demanded in a terrible voice.

Immediately, the man went into the barn to get the boots but the corpse would not accept them. "You will go to my grave and put them back on my feet again," he said.

And that was what he had to do but, after that, his koli lamp worked fine.

*This story came from the great Fetlar storyteller, Jamsie Laurenson.*

# 8

## The Goita Skerry

FOR a long time after Shetland became part of Scotland, Shetlanders continued to speak the old language and merchants traded with countries like Norway, Sweden, Denmark, the Baltic States and the Hanseatic league. One young Shetlander, a teenager, got a job on a ship that plied her trade across the North Sea.

After a time the young man was given some leave so he went home to the north of Yell to visit his parents. To his father he gave a knife as a present. The gleaming blade was razor sharp and it was set into a hardwood handle. It nestled in a leather sheath that was designed to be worn on a belt.

His father was delighted with the gift and he never allowed the knife out of his sight. He took a thin sweeing iron, heated it in the fire and burned his initials into the handle. This was to make sure that it would be his for all time. His wife said that he loved the knife more than he loved her.

One day, when he was out beachcombing, he saw a big bull seal sunbathing on a rock called the Goita Skerry. In those days seals were hunted, the skins were cured, the meat was eaten and the oil from the blubber was used to burn in the koli lamps.

The man drew his knife from its sheath and crept stealthily closer and closer to the sleeping seal. He made a lunge, full length, and stuck his knife into the animal. The seal, in the nick of time, realised his danger and desperately tried to get away from the man and the lethal knife.

Instead of being stabbed in the heart as the man intended, the knife struck deep into the seal's bony, sinewy flipper, near the top. The seal was big and strong and although he was wounded he was able to pull the knife from the man's grasp and disappear into the sea, leaving a trail of water that was discoloured by blood.

The man was not too worried by the loss of the seal, there were plenty of seals, but he was bitterly disappointed by the loss of his precious knife. Day after day he patrolled that area of coastline hoping to find the seal. Perhaps, he thought, the seal was so wounded that it would die and he would get back his knife.

Each day he drew a blank and in the end he had to accept that he was never going to get back his knife. Eventually he forgot about the seal and the knife, his son continued to sail on the same ship and came home to visit from time to time.

The young man had been at sea for about fourteen years, he was now fully matured, a fine man in every way, when he came home and had an exciting piece of news for his parents. He told them he was going to stay home for good and marry his childhood sweetheart.

His father, especially, was delighted to hear this. He was now getting old and he found the drudgery of the crofting harder and harder with each year that passed. His son also told him that he had ordered a new boat to be built for them. It was to be built by a family of Norwegians renowned for the quality of their workmanship. The boat would be completed over the winter, ready for collection in spring.

When the time came the two of them, father and son, made their way to Norway. When they got there they found that the new boat was, indeed, completed. Not only that, but it was exactly what they wanted, a boat to be proud of and they were impatient to get it back to Yell. Their departure from Norway was delayed, however, because of bad weather; severe gales from the north.

Norwegians are well known for their hospitality but the Yell men did not feel welcome in this household. There was no woman in the house, only two young men and their father. The two boys were the boat builders but it was clear that the father was the expert, the brains, and everything they did was under his supervision. The old Norwegian was severely crippled; he hobbled around, painfully, on a crutch.

He spoke little and he refused to make eye contact with any of his guests. The old Shetlander would be aware of the Norwegian staring at him but when he looked across the Norwegian would look away. They thought that maybe the time of year had something to do with it. It was May, all the winter food was eaten, it was too early for new crops and the weather made fishing impossible.

The weather did not relent; it was impossible to go to sea in a boat, so the hostile atmosphere had to be endured. One day, to try and make conversation, one of the Yell boys asked the Norwegians if they had made a boat for themselves.

The old Norwegian glared at him. "We have no need of a boat," he growled, before lapsing into a sullen silence.

The shortage of food became acute but the Norwegians seemed willing enough to share what little they had. Much to the Shetlanders' surprise, the old man, one morning, ordered his sons to go and catch them a fish. They had confessed to having no boat and besides, the weather was such that no boat could be launched. Without another word the two boys got up and left.

As the day wore on the old Norwegian started to get impatient when the boys failed to return. He hobbled his way to the door at regular intervals to look out and listen, but in vain. Darkness fell with no signs of the young men. None of them went to bed that night and at first light the father resumed his vigil in the doorway. It was a long anxious day but, at night, the boys finally reached home again.

"Where have you been?" their father demanded. "I have worried myself sick about you."

"Sorry, father," one of them said, "we didn't see a fish in the water until we were within sight of Shetland."

This simple statement told the Yell men a very great deal and did much to explain the unfriendly welcome that they had experienced. The Norwegians were seal people. They were of a race that could change from humans to seals and back again, at will.

Clearly they wanted to keep this a secret and they hoped that the Shetlanders would go before they found out the truth.

The boys had brought home a big beautiful cod, it was cooked for the supper and it was the best food any of them had tasted for many days. Now that the air had been cleared the Norwegians were much more friendly and, for the first time, they all talked freely. Seal folk were well known and understood by the Shetlanders and they were in no way alarmed by this revelation.

"Can I ask," said the old Yell man, "what happened? What kind of an accident did you have that made you so cripple?"

The old Norwegian slowly reached up the bare stone wall and put his hand into a recess, a blind window, and brought out a knife, which he handed over. It was the knife that had been given to the Shetlander by his son; the knife with his initials burned into the handle.

Referring to the blade, the old Norwegian said: "This is what you stuck into me on the Goita Skerry, all those years ago!"

*Sometimes my father would tell this as two separate stories, one of the recovery of the knife and the other about the fact that the sons had to go all the way to Shetland to find a fish.*

# 9

## Mees Kees

A LONG, long time ago there was a shipwreck on the Holm of Gloup – a small, green island that lies off the north coast of the island of Yell.

The holm has high, steep cliffs and anyone wanting to reach the top faces a hard climb. It has rich grass, a fresh water spring and for centuries farmers have raised a small number of quality lambs there. The top is domed so there is always shelter for the sheep. The sheep become very wild and they are very difficult to capture.

From the shipwreck three men survived, two of them were brothers by the name of Johnstone. They came originally from Ireland and they were stonemasons to trade. The third man was Dutch, his name was Mees Kees.

The three managed to scramble up to the top of the cliff but their plight was a very serious one. They had nothing but the clothes they stood up in and no way of protecting themselves from the cold. They had no food except the few limpets they could knock off the rocks, but the fresh water spring kept them from being thirsty.

In an attempt to attract attention from the shore they began to build a cairn. They gathered all the loose stones they could find and each day the cairn got higher and higher.

Each day the three men prayed for deliverance. They made a solemn pledge that if they survived they would show their gratitude by building a church. They had almost given up hope when, at last, they saw a boat heading towards them. The cairn had been noticed and they were, indeed, rescued.

It took some time for them to make a full recovery from their ordeal on the holm but as soon as they felt fit enough they set about the task of building the church that became known as the Kirk of Ness. They chose a site, in the north of Yell, near the loch that is now known as the Kirk Loch. Nearby is a smaller loch called Benewater. Its waters had long been regarded as holy because it was pure spring water. Benewater has no source of water other than from the earth.

The church was built from stone. The Johnstone brothers were skilled masons and progress was good. Local men worked with them as labourers, quarrying stones and helping in any way they could. One day, when the church was nearly finished, they were working on the roof when tragedy struck.

Mees Kees fell off the roof and broke his neck. He died instantly. The Johnstone brothers were grief stricken. They had been through a lot together and Mees Kees was a good friend. Mees Kees was buried close to the wall of the church and a wooden grave marker was erected at his head.

The church, however, was finished and used as a place of worship for more than two hundred years. It fell in to disuse and disrepair after the reformation but its surrounds are used as a burial ground to the present day. It is the cemetery for the whole of north Yell. The earth is clean and sandy, it overlooks the North Sea and it is adjacent to the beautiful beach of Breckon. Of the church itself there is little to be seen nowadays, it is a ruin and the walls are sunk down, deep among the sand.

There is a ruined croft house nearby, a house that had no near neighbours, called Toft. Some considerable time after the death of Mees Kees the man who lived in Toft was making a churn. He had the wood for the staves and the hoops but he had no piece of wood suitable for a bottom.

One day, when he was passing the graveyard, it occurred to him that Mees Kees' grave marker was exactly what he needed for a bottom for his churn. He returned at night, after everyone else had gone to bed, and he stole the grave marker of Mees Kees.

# Mees Kees

~ ~ ~

In his barn where he worked, he cut a circle from the wood which proved to be entirely suitable for the bottom of his churn. The churn was finally assembled and, after it was soaked in water, it was as tight as a drum.

The man from Toft was proud of his work and believed that the churn he had made would last a lifetime. His mind, however, was troubled. He knew that he was wrong to take the grave marker. He had stolen from the dead.

Once, in the middle of the night, an apparition appeared at his bedside. It was a frightening and ghostly figure and it spoke to the man from Toft in an awesome and chilling voice, "A'm Mees Kees an' A'm kum fur me trees," said the ghost.

The man from Toft was terrified and there was no more sleep for him that night. He knew that what he had seen was the ghost of Mees Kees demanding that his grave marker be returned. In the old Shetland dialect anything made from wood, especially any tool, was called a tree.

~ ~ ~

During the day the man from Toft convinced himself he had had a nightmare, and it would never happen again. He was wrong. The ghost of Mees Kees appeared every night and the awful voice would say, "A'm Mees Kees an' A'm kum fur me trees."

The man from Toft still had the remains of the grave marker in the barn and he considered ways and means of repairing it but it was ruined. Night after night the ghost haunted him and terrified him until he was demented by fear and the lack of sleep.

The man from Toft became so frightened that he never went to bed at all and he tried very hard to stay awake. He only slept when exhaustion overcame him. He knew that he would be driven to insanity unless he could find a way of satisfying Mees Kees. He began to search for another piece of wood that he could make into a grave marker.

He did not want to ask any of his neighbours because, if he did, he would have to tell them the whole story. To steal from the dead was well nigh unforgivable. If he confessed his sin he could become an outcast in the community. But he was desperate and he was forced to go from house to house and tell his story. It took many days and the man from Toft was in deep despair, but at last he was given a suitable piece of wood. He hurried home and began work on it.

He made it as near as he could to the same size and shape as the grave marker that he had stolen. When it was finished he took it to the graveyard. And so it was that Mees Kees, once again, had a stock at the head of his grave. After that the man from Toft was able to sleep easy in his bed and the ghost of Mees Kees never haunted him again.

*This is from my father. He had a great interest in the Kirk of Ness – for nearly forty years he looked after it and he was the gravedigger. He died in 1982 and he, too, is buried there.*

# 10

## The Selkie Boy of Breckon

IN THE north of the island of Yell there is a place called Breckon and, once upon a time, a very beautiful girl lived there. She had many admirers, indeed every young man in the village tried to woo her, but she would have none of it. One by one the young men gave up. They said that she was as cold as a fish.

One day the girl went to the beach to get some sand for the hens. There is, near Breckon, a geo where the sand is composed of crushed shells; it makes ideal grit for eggshells. She was so long away that her mother became worried. When she got back she told her mother that she had sat down by the shore and as it was a lovely warm day she had fallen asleep.

It was a big shock to the family when, a few months later, it became clear that the girl was expecting a baby. Her mother and father knew of no boyfriends, indeed they knew that she never wanted, or would have, a boyfriend. In the fullness of time she gave birth to a baby boy. However, it was no ordinary baby, he had webbed hands and feet and he was all covered in hair.

In the society of those days it was bad enough having a baby out of wedlock, but it was a thousand times worse to have such an abnormal child. The girl could give no explanation. She did not want to talk about it and her father was so angry and so frustrated that, in the end, he put her and the baby out of the house.

The girl and her child took shelter in a hovel nearby. They were cold, hungry and destitute, so much so that some nights they cried themselves to sleep.

One night the girl had a dream. She dreamed that if she went to the shore where she fell asleep and scraped among the sand she would find silver. The dream also told her that the silver was really for the boy, not for her, but because the boy still needed her so much she could have some too. She was warned in the dream never to be greedy, she was to take just enough silver for their needs and no more.

She went to the geo the very next day and she did, indeed, find silver. She did exactly as the dream instructed and only took a small amount. She made regular trips to the shore when she had need, and always found silver.

This went on until the boy was twelve years old, when he went to the sea. He was always more seal than human and the sea was his natural home. He was never seen on shore again and his mother never saw him again. She was still very poor but, no matter how often she went to the shore, she never found silver again. But the place has been known as Silver Geo ever since.

*I heard this story from my father and also from the late Andrew Williamson of the Brake, Cullivoe, when I was a child.*

# 11

## The Gold Cradle

IN BYGONE days when a young couple married they usually lived together with one set of parents. One such couple lived with the bridegroom's parents. At first they all lived happily together but as time went on tensions began to appear. The woman of the house, as she got old, lost her eyesight and her husband became very cripple, he could only sit beside the fire.

The young couple had no children. This made them very unhappy and it became an obsession with the young wife. She would mope around and do little of the work. They were very poor and the burden of putting food on the table was totally the responsibility of the young man. Towards the end of one summer he was at his wit's end to know how they were going to survive the coming winter.

The only food they had for the winter was a field of potatoes that he had carefully tended. The potatoes had reached the stage where they were almost ready to harvest but one day, when he went to the field to get some for the dinner, he found that they were rotten. In panic he went to all parts of the field and lifted a shaw every here and there. It was no good, they were all black and pulpy and useless.

The young man was heartbroken. He sat down on a stone, his head in his hands and the tears rolling down his face. "What will we do, what will we do?" he sobbed.

He was aware of someone beside him and when he looked up he saw a tiny little man, a trow. The trow asked why it was that he was in the depths of despair so he told him the story of how it was at home. His mother was blind, his father was a cripple and his wife was obsessed by the fact that they had no family. Now they had lost their potato crop and they faced starvation in the winter.

"I would like to help you," said the trow, "but the truth is that this is a bad time for us too. I would like to give you three wishes but right now all that I can offer you is the one wish."

The young man thanked the trow and asked, in some alarm, if he had to make the wish immediately.

"No, no," replied the trow. "You have to make the wish within twenty-four hours. Meet me here at this time tomorrow and remember that you have one wish and one wish only."

With that the trow disappeared and the young man made his weary way home and told his family the story of the day's events.

"Well," said his mother, "there's only the one wish that you can make and that is to get back my eyesight. None of you have any idea how bad it is to be blind, so let that be your wish."

The young wife did not agree. "I mean you no disrespect mother, but you are old now, you have had your day," she said. "We have to look to the future, we must wish for a baby boy. If we had a baby boy not only will he bring us great joy but he will grow quickly and he will work and bring money to the house."

"Nonsense," shouted the old man, "a child in the house now would be yet another mouth to feed and it will be years before he can grow up enough to help us, we will be dead from hunger by that time. But I do agree with you on one point, we old folk have had our day and it does not matter what happens to us."

Looking to his son, he went on, "You have to wish for gold. If we have gold then we can buy food and the things we need. I know that gold cannot buy youth, eyesight, nor yet can it buy me a grandson, but gold is the only sensible thing to wish for."

The young man listened to all this in silence but with mounting anger. "You are all so selfish," he said. "It is I who has been given the wish and I have held this house together for years and yet you never, for a moment, consider my feelings or what I may want to wish for."

# The Gold Cradle

~ ~ ~

They all asked him what he was going to wish for but he gave no answer except to say that he would sleep on it and make up his mind in the morning.

When morning came they asked him again but he was no more forthcoming. "I have made up my mind. I know what I am going to wish for, but I will say no more, you will all know soon enough if my wish is granted."

So saying, he went off to meet the trow. The trow appeared again as he had promised and asked the young man if he wanted to make a wish. He said yes, and the trow warned him, yet again, that he only had the one wish. The trow invited him to make the wish now.

"I wish that my mother can see my baby son being rocked in a gold cradle," he said.

*I first heard this story from Marion Craig. She told it in Gaelic when we were both storytellers at an Isle of Skye festival. She later told it in English, that is how I learned it, but I also heard it from another storyteller, Liz Weir in Cushendall, Ireland.*

# 12

## The Backstone

GLOUP is the most northerly village on the island of Yell. Prior to 1881 the beach at Nethertoon in Gloup was the site of a big, important haaf fishing station. The haaf fishing was hard, dangerous work. It was so called because the word haaf means distant or far. Men would sail or row open boats called sixtreens - six oared boats - as much as forty miles off shore to the fishing grounds.

At the fishing grounds, on the edge of the continental shelf, long lines baited with cockles were set. Each boat would have several lines and when the lines were hauled in the catch was taken on board. The fish that they wanted were mostly ling and cod. Sometimes they would stay at sea for several days and they would take to sea with them a fire kettle and some food, often milk and oatcakes.

The boats were owned by the merchants and the landowners. Fishermen were compelled to fish for the owners of the boats and they were obliged to sell the fish caught to the same people at whatever price they offered. Fishermen and their families lived on crofts where they had no security of tenure. Lairds could evict a tenant at any time. Prices in the shops were rigged, so that the poor people were constantly in debt and, therefore, beholden to the merchants and lairds.

On the shore at fishing stations like Nethertoon, the fish were cleaned, washed, split, salted and dried in the sun. Boys, too young to be fisherman, were given the task of looking after the fish. Every morning they would lay out the fish on the beach. At intervals the fish were turned over so that they dried evenly.

If there was any sign of rain the fish were taken inside but put out again whenever it stopped raining. The owners of the fish would store it until the time was right to sell. Most of it was exported to continental Europe, to Catholic countries where they had the tradition of eating fish every Friday.

Some fish caught, like halibut and turbot, did not lend themselves to salting so they were of little value. Such fish made superb eating for the local folk but sometimes halibut and turbot were so plentiful that they were laid down on the beach and the boats were hauled up over them. The slime and oil from the rich fish greased the keels of the boats. Sometimes the merchants would keep one or two pigs to eat the waste fish and offal.

The haaf fishing was essentially a summer activity; winter weather and the short days made it impossible for boats to venture so far from the shore. Some inshore fishing took place in the wintertime using smaller, lighter boats. They fished for haddocks, whiting and other white fish whenever the weather allowed.

Every haaf fishing station had buildings called lodges. They were usually crude stone-built houses that were used by fishermen who lived so far away from the station that walking home each night was impossible. Men would live and sleep in the lodges, only going home at the weekends during the summer fishing season. During the winters the lodges were bare and empty but each year they were spring cleaned and made ready for the summer season.

One boat's crew, when they returned to Nethertoon for the summer season, found that the backstone from the lodge was missing. To them it was no big deal. The backstone was simply a large flat stone set on its edge for the fire to burn against. One of the men found another suitable stone and no one thought any more of it. They got on with the business of preparing for the summer haaf fishing season.

The long lines had thousands of hooks and they all had to be baited. At sea they cut up any low value fish they caught, but ashore the two main baits used were cockles and sand eels. Bastavoe was a rich source of cockles. A well trodden path spanned Gloup Voe and Bastavoe. The path passed through Heatherdale, a beautiful lonely valley with hardly anyone living there.

Surprisingly, Heatherdale boasted a shop. It was owned and run by Mr Pole. He owned the boats working out of Nethertoon and he was known as a hard, miserly man who had no compassion for the plight of the fishermen and crofters who lived in dire poverty. Pole's shop stocked all the goods that the fishermen needed, food and fishing tackle. No fisherman would have dared to buy anything elsewhere.

The other source of bait came from the beautiful Sands of Breckon, about two miles south of Gloup. At low tide it was possible to draw sand eels. A blunt sickle or a length of stiff wire was pushed down through the sand, the fisher walked backwards, the wriggling of the eels could be felt on the sickle and it would be pulled quickly but smoothly upwards to the surface. If the sickle was pulled up too hard the eels would be cut in half and if the eels were not picked up immediately they would, in an instant, disappear down through the sand again.

This was another job that the beach boys might get sent to do. Schoolboys gathered bait too. It might be before school or after school, depending on the state of the tide. Sometimes women helped with the baiting of lines. The gathering of the bait, cutting it up and putting a piece on each and every hook was a long, time consuming and tedious chore.

In the morning, with baited lines, food and fire kettle, the crew who had lost the backstone drew down the sixteen and left Nethertoon bound for the far haaf. Other boats left at the same time, all glad to be back at sea after the long winter and the monotony of the salt meat and salt fish that had, for so long, been their diet.

The men who had lost their backstone caught no fish. They were the only unlucky boat; many of the others had big catches. It was a disappointment for them but nothing all that unusual. Sometimes a boat would have, for no known reason, a bad spell. This boat, however, had so little fishing luck and caught so little fish that even the oldest of the fishermen could not remember anything like it happening before.

# The Backstone

~ ~ ~

The bad luck went on for weeks on end and the men began to get disheartened. They began to question whether it was worth the effort of baiting and setting lines only to haul them in again with the bait gone.

"What are we going to do about Johnsmas?" asked the youngest crewman, timidly.

"Johnsmas," snarled an older man, "how can we hold Johnsmas. We have caught no fish, our debt with Pole is getting bigger by the day, what have we to hold Johnsmas with?"

The skipper thought for a moment. "I have been fishing for nigh on fifty years," he said. "I have never seen a year yet that we did not have a Johnsmas foy and we will have Johnsmas this year too."

Johnsmas, the feast day of St John, is the 25th of June and it was the most important day in the fisherman's calendar. No fishing was done that day, it was a day of feasting, drinking, music making and dancing.

One of the crew was John Omand of Vigon. Vigon is the most north-westerly corner of Yell; nowadays it is completely empty of people. John Omand's father, James, had a reputation as a spaeman, a warlock. He could do more than maet himself as people politely said. James Omand was old, feeble and housebound but when he heard of the missing backstone and the total lack of success of the boat he sent for Robbie Nicholson to come and see him.

Robbie was another of the crew. James Omand knew that to send for his own son was useless because John despised his father's magic. He would have no truck with this mumbo jumbo. Robbie Nicholson had great respect for James Omand so he made his way to Vigon at the very first opportunity.

The old man was full of questions. He wanted to know if it was true that they were catching no fish and if it was true that someone had stolen their backstone. When Robbie was able to confirm all this James lapsed into deep thought.

"Do you know who took the backstone?" he asked.

"We have a pretty good idea," replied Robbie.

"Well," said James, "the first thing that you have to do is get it back. It does not matter how you do it; you can go and ask for it, you can take it back by stealth, but get it back you must, even if you have to fight for it. When you get it back put it in the lodge where it belongs and make preparations for the haaf as usual."

James paused for thought. "When you go off you might still not catch any fish. If that is the case do not stay off too long, come ashore again. When you come to the beach turn the boat around so that you come in to the beach stern first and pull it up far enough so that the nile is clear of the water. You have to stay in the boat, Robbie, but sit looking out to sea and wait until one of the crew brings you something to eat and something to drink.

"When you have finished the food and drink," James continued, and then paused, "you have to make water. Pee out through the nile hole but after that behave as normal, bait the lines, set them and you will get fish, I promise."

Robbie made his way back to Nethertoon in a very thoughtful frame of mind. He reported his meeting with James Omand to the skipper and he wondered what the reaction might be. The skipper took the view that there was nothing to be lost by carrying out James's instructions. He made the point that they were getting no fish anyway so there was nothing to be lost.

They found the backstone and returned it to its proper place, baited the lines and set them the following day. They caught very little but James had suggested that this might happen. When they returned to the beach they followed James's instructions to the letter. The lines were reset and this time, for the first time in the summer, they were heavy with fish.

Their luck had totally changed and day after day they had bigger landings than any other boat out of Gloup. The biggest day of all came in August when they landed the heaviest catch ever recorded in Nethertoon, a record. At the end of that haaf fishing season they made up all the lost ground and they paid off with more money than any other boat. Even the most sceptical had respect for the spaeman from Vigon, James Omand.

*I heard my father tell this story to the late Bertie Henderson of West-A-Firth in February 1955 when the two of them were clearing snow from the road to Gloup.*

# 13

## Coul

WHEN Christianity first came to Shetland the newly converted people of south Unst wanted to build a church to worship in. The priest, with powerful missionary zeal, encouraged them in their efforts. A site was chosen and the work of quarrying suitable stones began. The best stonemasons in the area were gathered together and building, inspired with hope and faith, began.

On the first day they put in foundation stones but the following morning they were dismayed to find that all their hard work had been undone. Some of the biggest stones had disappeared altogether and some others had been put back into the earth. It did not take the priest long to come to the conclusion that the trows were responsible for the destruction of the foundations.

The trows were the 'little people' who lived in the hill. They were seldom seen but they had some potent magic. Normally the trows were easy going and they hardly ever disturbed humans, but for some unknown reason they hated Christianity. It was true that the priest did not like them and he often, in a loud voice, preached against them and put curses on them, their spells and their cantrips.

Undeterred, the priest and the men of south Unst resumed work, but again the trows tore down everything that they built. And so it was, day after day, the men working through the daytime and the trows at night. The trows looked like winning this battle of wills

but the priest declared that he was going to put a stop to the destructive activities of the trows.

The priest urged the builders to even greater efforts and he pledged himself to guard the site and he would defy the trows from so much as touching a single stone. All that day the men worked with renewed vigour, they had the utmost faith in the ability of their leader to quell the disruptive and troublesome trows. The next morning they gathered feeling certain that they were making real progress.

Imagine their total dismay when they found that the site had been levelled and no trace of their labours was to be seen. Worse still, they found a short distance away, the priest, dead. The trows had killed him. The community was so dispirited that no further attempt was made at building a church. They had to admit that the trows were too strong for them and some thought that, perhaps, Christianity was not such a good idea after all.

The holiest man in all Shetland lived in the north of Unst. His name was Coul. Not only was he a preacher but he was also a powerful healer. Coul had become very old and feeble, he walked with difficulty and he was so stooped that his long white beard hung down to his knees. Nonetheless, he journeyed the length of the island to try to heal a sick child who lived in Uyeasound.

Coul was very angry when he was told of the battle between the priest and the trows. He scolded the men of south Unst for being so weak and defeatist as to give in to the trows. He ordered that work on the church should recommence at once. He said that he would guard the site during the nights and declared that the trows would never dare kill or harm him.

The following morning their work, yet again, had been undone and Coul had disappeared. As it turned out, the trows had taken him prisoner. Coul's reputation had deterred the trows from killing him. Although they hated Coul they did not want his death on their conscience so they kept him in a sea cave at the back of the Bluemull.

After Coul had been in this damp, cold cave for five weeks the trows saw plainly that he was going to die. He was so old and weak that he would not last long. The trows reasoned that if Coul died while he was their prisoner then they were fully responsible for his death, as surely as if they had killed him at the church site. So Coul was released.

Slowly and painfully, Coul made his way north towards his home, but so feeble and ill was he that he collapsed and died at a place called Yella Brun. At the place where Coul fell, spring water appeared and the beautiful clear cool water flows to this day. It is said that the water has all the same healing powers that Coul himself had.

*I was told this story in the Heritage Centre in Haroldswick. Several ladies told me the story at the same time, the only time that I heard a story told by a committee!*

# 14

## The Red Roses

THERE was once a preacher who fell in love with a young girl who lived in his parish. She was very fond of him too and in the fullness of time he proposed marriage to her. She accepted but she had a big problem. She knew that her husband wanted, more than anything, to have children.

She did not have the courage to tell him that she had a terrible fear of becoming pregnant and especially of childbirth. She lay awake at night wondering what she could do to avoid having children and the night before the wedding she had a dream.

She dreamed that if she went to the mill and turned the millstone backwards, anti-clockwise one turn, that would prevent conception. It was a vivid dream and the following morning she rose early and went to the mill.

She made sure that no one saw her and she did what the dream suggested, but to be certain, she turned the millstone backwards three revolutions. This done, she went back to the house to prepare for her big day.

The wedding went as planned. All the parishioners were there to partake in the wedding feast and they all wished the happy couple well and expressed the hope that they would be blessed by a large and healthy family.

In the months that followed the young couple were very happy and they enjoyed the popularity that they had. However, as time went on without any sign of a child on the way, things gradually changed. The preacher began to look at his wife with accusing eyes.

One evening, when they were out for a walk, things came to a head. The sun was still bright but it was low in the sky and the shadows were long. With their backs to the sun the preacher's shadow stretched away out in front of them, but he stopped in his tracks in horror when he saw that his wife cast no shadow at all.

"What have you done?" he demanded, angrily.

"What do you mean?" his wife asked, timidly.

"You cast no shadow and this can only mean that you have committed some dreadful sin. What is this evil thing that you have done woman?"

Immediately her mind went back to the morning of their wedding when she had rotated the millstone. She knew that he would be furious if she told him so she refused to tell him anything and, indeed, denied that she had done anything wrong.

"I must know what you have done," he replied grimly. "One way or another I will get the truth out of you."

That night he locked her in the church and vowed that she would tell him the truth in the morning. She was terrified when she heard the key grind the lock shut and she sank down on the floor sobbing. Without knowing it she fell sound asleep and she had a frightening dream.

With her in the cold, dark, empty church was a white ram with a black head. Gradually the ram became more and more real and he spoke to her in an awful voice. "If you had allowed me to be conceived, if you had allowed me to be born, I would have grown into a distinguished man. I would have become a judge at the high court but it never happened because of your evil work in the mill."

So saying, the ram backed off before charging at the girl with his head lowered and his huge horns in front. He hit her with brutal force and knocked her flat on the floor and whenever she tried to get up he knocked her flat again.

When she stopped trying to rise, the ram hooked her dress on one of his horns and dragged her around the church, deliberately crashing her head and body against the rigid wooden pews. When morning came at last she was black and blue all over and utterly exhausted.

Her husband took her out of the church demanding to know what had happened through the night but she told him nothing. She crawled into bed and lay there weeping. The preacher showed no sympathy or compassion for her condition. All through the day he asked questions and demanded answers.

She steadfastly refused to tell him anything, so in the evening, ignoring her pleading and weeping, he took her and roughly pushed her in through the church door and again turned the key so that she had no chance of getting out. Now she was even more terrified because she knew what to expect.

She fought hard to stay awake but at length exhaustion closed her eyes and the dream came back to her. This time it was a different ram, it was black with a white collar. It spoke to her in the same awful voice as the other ram had done the night before. "If you had allowed me to be conceived, if you had allowed me to be born, I would have grown into a very distinguished man. I would have become the archbishop but it never happened because of your evil work in the mill."

The ram began to butt and drag her around the church and if the ram on the first night was cruel and vicious then this one was even worse. By morning she was so badly hurt that she was unable to walk unaided. Her husband helped her into bed and again questioned her pitilessly, but again she told him nothing.

In the evening she was unable to get up but her husband was merciless. "If you are so wicked that you will not tell the truth then you will have to suffer accordingly."

With that he opened the church door and threw her in. She landed with a cry of severe pain from her bruised and battered

# The Red Roses

~ ~ ~

body. So deep in despair was she that she no longer cared what happened to her but, as before, she fell asleep and this time she had a very different dream.

This time it was not a ram; it was a tragic little girl. She was ugly and horribly deformed but she came to the preacher's wife and spoke to her in a soft gentle voice. "You did not allow me to be conceived, you never allowed me to be born, and for that I thank you from the bottom of my heart. I am so grateful that I do not have to go out into the world with a body like this."

The wife slept little during the rest of the night but the sad little girl had moved her in a way that the violence of the rams never could. In the morning her husband had to carry her out of the church but this time she broke down and confessed. She told him the whole story.

She asked for his forgiveness but he was furious and told her that for her sins she would rot in hell. As she lay helpless on the bed she asked again, "When will I be forgiven?"

The preacher pointed to her shoes, which had been discarded on the floor of the bedroom. "You will be forgiven when the laces of your shoes grow into red roses," he replied.

With a groan she sank back in the bed, so broken was she in both mind and body that she died a few days later. A coffin was made for her and she was sealed inside. It was left in the bedroom until the funeral could be arranged.

The preacher did not want to conduct the funeral service himself so there was a considerable delay before a minister from another parish was available. When the men went into the bedroom to remove the coffin they were astonished to see that the shoes on the floor were both full of red roses.

*I heard this story, told in Faroese, at a storytelling night on the island of Sandoy. Deep into the same night, with glasses of Orkney whisky in our hands, my Faroese friend Katrine Pederson translated it for me.*

# 15

## The Trows' Boats

IT WAS Saturday morning so Nancy did not have to go to school, but it was also cold, windy and raining so not much good for playing outside either. Nancy was having breakfast and beside her was one of her favourite people in the whole world, her grandad.

Grandad was visiting on his way home from doing one of his favourite hobbies, beachcombing. Whenever the wind was strong and blowing onshore, grandad liked to walk along the beach looking for driftwood. Because there are no trees in Shetland sea-driven wood is very important to the Shetland folk.

Nancy finished her boiled egg and pushed the egg cup with the empty shell away from her. Grandad took the spoon and punched a hole in the shell.

"Why did you do that, grandad?" asked Nancy.

"So that the trows can't use it for a boat," he replied. "The first trows that ever came to Shetland came in an eggshell."

"They had to be very small trows," remarked Nancy.

"All trows are small," grandad told her, "but if you want I will tell you the whole story."

Nancy's mother smiled to herself. She was doing her housework and she knew that her seven-year-old loved grandad's stories. She poured her father another cup of tea and he began.

Once upon a time all the trows in the world lived on an island far away in a place called Pirniewick. They were carefree and as happy as the day is long. They used to grow vegetables and fruit.

# The Trows' Boats
~ ~ ~

They made wine, they kept bees and had honey, and they loved to sing and dance and play their fiddles. They knew magic too but some things were beyond them. They could not cross salt water and they had no boats. This meant that they could not leave Pirniewick, but so happy were they that they did not want to leave anyway.

Happy, that is, until the Kalathumpians arrived. They were as big and ugly as the trows were small and dainty. The Kalathumpians were bad tempered; they were monsters and bullies.

They stole all the nice things that the trows owned and they trampled flat all their crops with their big hobnailed boots. Now the trows were sad and miserable. Each and every one of them went around with faces as if they had stood up before their faces were set.

To make matters worse, every Halloween the Kalathumpians could make themselves seven times bigger than normal; and seven times as bad tempered. The biggest of them all was a man called Hostra. He was so big that he measured nine inches between his eyes and he was four and twenty knuckles from the spoon of his chest to the knot of his trapple. The little trows were terrified of him; he destroyed everything in his path.

~ ~ ~

The trows could change size at Halloween too, but it was no use making themselves bigger because they were still far smaller than the Kalathumpians. So, by contrast, they would make themselves far smaller, so small that they were no bigger than mooratoogs and they could hide in the cracks of the walls. Here they were safe until Hostra and the others returned to normal.

One day, when Hostra was in an extra bad mood, he kicked the hen house over the cliff. Most of the hens survived because they were outside at the time but, to the trows, this was the last straw. They decided that they had to get away. They could no longer live with the Kalathumpians.

So they used all their magic to make themselves as small as possible and the hens as big as possible so that they laid huge eggs. The eggs were so big that the trows could use the shells for boats and that is how they came to Shetland.

"Are they still here, grandad?" asked Nancy.

"That they are, more's the pity my lamb, yon hill folk can work a lot of spoiley," replied grandad.

"Maybe it's you that keeps them here," Nancy told him.

"How do you make that out?" demanded grandad.

"Because, if you break all the eggshells, maybe they can't get away again!"

*I wrote this story. It is based on the belief that eggshells were used by the trows as boats.*

# 16

## The Man Who Drowned in Greth

ONCE upon a time there was a woman who had the gift of second sight. She did not have full control; she did not always know what was going to happen, but every now and then she would be aware of a forthcoming event and she usually knew if someone was about to die.

Her husband was a fisherman. They were a happy couple but they had no children. One day the knowledge came to her that her husband was going to drown. She told him but he scoffed at the idea and he refused to stay home from the fishing, he had no belief in his wife's gift of second sight.

Desperate to keep her man away from the sea she hatched a plan. They had, in those days, no alarm clocks. Fishermen responded to the morning light; as soon as the dawn broke they went to sea.

When they went to bed that night the woman stayed awake and waited for her husband to fall into a sound sleep. She got up in the middle of the night and very carefully blacked out the window with heavy, dark coloured blankets.

The man's body clock worked as usual but when he awoke and could see no light at the window he turned over and went back to sleep again. When next he wakened he needed the toilet, so he got up and made his way to the greth sae – the big wooden tub that they gathered urine in. The urine was used to waak (shrink) the wadmil (homemade tweed).

~ ~ ~

In the pitch dark the fisherman tripped over boots left on the floor, fell head first into the sae of greth, and was drowned.

*This is a story well known in Orkney and elsewhere. I like the story because of the 'what will be, will be' aspect.*

# 17

## Peerie Merron

ON THE north coast of the island of Yell is the Sands of Breckon. It is the most beautiful sandy beach in Shetland. It has clean, golden sand, and surf rolling in that ranges in colour between deep, dark blue and snow white.

To the east is Silver Geo – a coarse beach of big boulders. At the end of the beach is the Johannagroat Hole where the sand is composed of crushed shells; many whole beautiful shells can be found.

In between the Sands of Breckon and Silver Geo is the Ness of Houlland, a long arm of land that sticks out into the North Sea. The ness is broken into three parts, with deep yeas that can be difficult to cross, and the sea runs through the outer one. The last bit of the ness is a rock, off the end, called the Burravoe Kist.

It is said that it was the trows that placed the Ness of Houlland where it is. The trows wanted to make a bridge across Yell Sound and the ness was to be part of the bridge. They had fetched the ness from some place away in the east but when they came to north Yell they needed a rest so they set it down while they had breakfast.

It was porridge for breakfast and each of the trows was given a big, wooden bowlful. A little girl called Merron was the youngest, smallest and weakest of all the trows. She was given porridge the same as all the rest but she had no spoon. The leader of the trows noticed this and he said in a loud voice:

*"Caa fast an sup shune*
*Fur Peerie Merron wants a spoon."*

The trows were all very hungry and they soon gobbled up their breakfast, but they were also impatient and they wanted to get on with the work. They all forgot about Peerie Merron; she never got a spoon and she never got breakfast. The trows lifted up the ness again to transport it onward but Peerie Merron was so tired and so weak that she was unable to take her share of the burden.

She collapsed under the strain and she brought down all the rest with her. The ness itself hit the ground so hard that it broke into three pieces, the way it still is today. It was no more use for a bridge and the trows had no more use for it so they never lifted it up again.

*Yet another story that I heard from my father when I was a child.*

# 18

## Jan Tait and the Bear

WHEN Shetland was a part of Norway the king, each year, sent his chamberlain to collect the skat, as taxes were called in those days. The udallers were the tenants, the small farmers, who occupied the land. Each and every one of them was obliged to pay tax.

The skat could be paid in many different ways. Money was, of course, readily accepted, but if a farmer had no money then he was allowed to pay with farm produce, butter, cheese, meal, wool or tweed – all regarded as suitable currency.

When the tax gatherer arrived on the island of Fetlar he set up his headquarters at a place called Urie. One of the udallers who came to offer payment was a young man called Jan Tait. He was big and strong and had his bare chest and bare feet. Anyone who saw Jan Tait for the first time quickly noticed his feet.

Jan Tait's feet were big and incredibly ugly. They were covered in lumps, bunions and corns. Running through them were thick, knotted veins and the toenails were black and broken. After walking through wet moorland they were none too clean either. Jan Tait was bold and direct. He announced, loudly, that he would pay his skat with butter.

The chamberlain weighed the butter on his bismar, a simple device used in ancient times. It consisted of a pole, about a metre long, with a standard weight on one end and a hook on the other end. Jan Tait's butter was suspended from the hook, the point of balance on a beam indicated the weight.

After studying the bismar the tax gatherer declared that it was insufficient, more butter was needed for full payment. He even accused Jan Tait of trying to cheat him. Jan Tait had his own bismar and he knew that the butter he had brought was the correct amount. He quickly realised that it was the chamberlain who was dishonest and a furious quarrel ensued.

Jan Tait was hot tempered and when the tax gatherer accused him of dishonesty it was more than he could bear. He struck the chamberlain a violent blow on the head with the heavy end of the bismar and he fell dead at Jan Tait's ugly feet. Immediately he regretted his fit of rage, but it was too late, the deed was done.

It was not that unusual for men to be killed in fights. There was little or no law in those days. When one man killed another, if he showed proper remorse or paid compensation to the victim's family, then the authorities would take no interest in the matter. Jan Tait's case was very different. He had killed the king's chamberlain. It was looked on as a direct challenge to the Crown, an act of treason.

Jan Tait was arrested and taken to Bergen in Norway, where the king had established his capital. He was neither bound nor chained and, surprisingly, he was allowed to retain the short-handled axe that he always had with him. He was led in to appear before the king to be sentenced. His guilt was never in doubt and the only appropriate punishment for murdering the king's chamberlain was death.

The king was seated on his throne surrounded by his officers, aides and the ladies of the court. The leader of the guards escorting Jan Tait described his crime and the circumstances of it to the king and everyone waited for the royal verdict. Like everyone else, the king's eyes were drawn to Jan Tait's feet. To universal murmurs and nods of agreement the king declared them to be the ugliest of feet in the whole world.

"If my feet offend your majesty then I shall try to make them look better."

So saying, Jan Tait took up his axe and began to chop off the lumps from his feet. The big, horrible lumps were rolling under the king's throne and there was blood, skin and toenails everywhere.

# Jan Tait and the Bear

~ ~ ~

"Stop, stop," shouted the king. "You are making it ten times worse. In fact I think I'm going to be sick. All the same," he added, "when a man has so little regard for his own flesh and blood it comes as no surprise that he lost his temper with a dishonest tax gatherer."

The king sat silent for a time, deep in thought. At last he came to his conclusion. "It would be a great pity to put to death such a young, strong, brave man. Jan Tait, I am going to give you an opportunity to earn a pardon. There is a bear living in the forest near here, he causes fear and alarm among my tenants and honest folk are afraid to leave their homes at night for fear of attack."

After a further pause for thought, the king went on, "The bear is a thief. He steals everything that my tenants produce from the land. If they have milk he steals that, if they make butter or cheese he steals that, if they grow fruit he steals that. Some of them keep bees and the bear steals the honey. Jan Tait, if you want to live this is what you must do. Capture the bear and bring him to me, alive. If you do that I will allow you to go back to Fetlar, a free man."

The king dismissed Jan Tait from the royal presence. One of the aides showed him a path that led to the edge of the forest. When Jan Tait entered the forest he found himself in a totally alien environment. He was from Shetland, from Fetlar, and never before had he seen or touched a tree. The sounds of the forest he found strange and weird. He could not see the way ahead and he had been in the forest no time at all until he was hopelessly lost.

He wandered aimlessly the rest of the day. He was cold and hungry and he could not even find his way out of the forest again. He knew nothing about bears either and he had no confidence in his own ability to overpower the bear should he encounter it. From what he had heard, this bear was a very big, strong and dangerous animal. Jan Tait's mind was in turmoil, he hardly knew whether he wanted to find the bear or not.

It was early evening and dusk was falling when Jan Tait discovered a clearing. He was very disconsolate. He was in despair. With a deep groan he sat down on a fallen tree and held his head in his hands. After a time, an old woman came into the clearing. She was gathering firewood and at first she was frightened of Jan Tait, he did have a wild unkempt appearance.

Jan Tait told her who he was and why he was in the forest. The old woman knew all about the bear. The bear had stolen from her and her husband and she was hurrying to get home before dark. The bear was usually on the prowl and she was frightened that he saw her.

The old lady was sympathetic towards Jan Tait and his plight. She, too, had to pay taxes and she knew that some of the tax gatherers were corrupt. She invited Jan Tait to her home to meet her husband. It was a beautifully made wooden cabin in another clearing. The cabin was very small so, after giving Jan Tait food, they made up a bed for him in the barn, among the fresh smelling hay.

The next morning during breakfast, and after a really good night's sleep, the old woman said, "I have a plan. Butter got you into this fix so maybe butter can get you out of it."

She asked her husband to help Jan Tait. She wanted the two men to make ropes that were strong enough to tie up the bear. They went back to the barn and began to wind straw into suitable cord. In the meantime she took a big tub and went among the neighbours, gathering from them all the butter they could give her.

By the time she returned with her butter tub nearly full the men had a good long length of rope made. After lunch, she guided Jan Tait to a path that she said the bear often used. After she had gone home again Jan Tait put down the tub of butter on the path and, with his rope, he climbed a tree to wait for the bear to make an appearance.

After a long wait – it was nearly dark again – the bear, grunting loudly, came lumbering along the path.

The bear homed in immediately on the butter and began to eat it greedily. Jan Tait had been told that the bear's favourite food was butter. Seeing the speed and the relish with which he scoffed the tubful it was entirely believable. In no time at all, the tub was empty and the bear put in his head and licked out every last trace of the butter.

The bear yawned sleepily, stretched out on the earth, and fell fast asleep. He was in a very deep sleep (maybe the old woman put something in the butter to make him sleep). Jan Tait jumped down from the tree and, as quickly as he could, he tied up the bear. The

bear wakened, but he was too late. Jan Tait had him secured, especially his jaws; the bear's teeth looked frighteningly healthy and strong.

When he was satisfied that the bear could not escape Jan Tait made his way back to the cabin to tell his friends that he had captured the bear. The news spread like wildfire and six men came forward offering help in taking the bear to the king. They carried the bear most of the way to the palace before Jan Tait ordered that the bear's hind legs be released so that he could walk.

They rigged tethers on either side of the bear's head and two strong men prevented the bear from sheering off to either side. Another man was behind the bear, with a stick, to prod him along and keep him moving. Jan Tait himself led the procession and, bold as brass, marched into the palace, into the throne room and straight up in front of the king, announcing loudly that he had brought, as ordered, the bear to the royal presence.

The king was very taken aback. For him this was totally unexpected, he believed that the bear would kill Jan Tait and that Jan Tait would no longer be a problem. In his mind Jan Tait richly deserved to die, after all he was a murderer and should not go unpunished.

His thoughts were interrupted by the sound of Jan Tait's voice. "Your majesty," he said, "I have brought you the bear, now can I go home to Fetlar?"

The king was about to say no, but all his aides and others were quick to remind him of his promise.

Reluctantly, he agreed that Jan Tait could go, but told him that he had to take the bear with him. "It will be a bad day for you, Jan Tait, if I ever see you or the bear again," he added, darkly.

Jan Tait did not have to be told twice to leave the palace but he still had the problem of the bear. Of course, he could have killed the bear, the bear was at his mercy, but this he would not do. Jan Tait felt that the bear had saved his life and that it would be entirely wrong to harm him. To release the bear again was out of the question so there was nothing else for it; he took the bear home with him to Fetlar.

In Fetlar the people were surprised and delighted to see Jan Tait. The killing of the crooked chamberlain had made him something of a folk hero. When he was arrested and taken to Norway no one ever expected to see him again, but here he was, alive and well, albeit his feet looked slightly different.

However, there was no welcome for the bear. The udallers of Fetlar were very hostile to the bear and threatened to kill him. They believed that the bear would be as disruptive in Fetlar as he was in Norway, and they told Jan Tait, in no uncertain terms, that the bear had to go. They would not tolerate him under any circumstances. Jan Tait, even now, would not harm the bear.

And so it was that Jan Tait tethered the bear on the uninhabited island of Lingy. Lingy lies in the triangle formed by the bigger islands of Unst, Yell and Fetlar. Needless to say, the bear was unhappy and he constantly tramped round and round at his tether's end. Being a big heavy animal he marked the soft earth and made a circular path that can still be seen to this day.

*This is the first story I ever learned. It is so long ago that I have no recollection of the first time I heard it, it is as if I have always had it; but it came from my father.*

# 19

## The Woolly Horse

THERE was once a farmer who lived in a remote area. His wife had died some time ago and he lived with his two grown up sons and a housekeeper. The farmer was known as a very tight fisted man, someone who never spent money unless there was no alternative.

It was autumn. All the crops were harvested and the stock from the farm had been sold. The only things left to do were the preparations for the oncoming winter. The farmer and his family were almost self-sufficient in food. The farm provided them with vegetables and meat.

Despite the season the weather was good; a beautiful Indian summer. The farmer rounded up and slaughtered eight sheep to be salted for winter meat. Later in the day the farmer and his sons made a rare journey to the nearest shop to buy salt, flour, oatmeal and other essential supplies.

The two sons yoked their horse in the gig. This was not an easy job as the horse was young and not fully broken to harness. As they started on the six-mile trip the farmer decided that this was an ideal opportunity to run some of the fire out of the horse. They set him off at a brisk pace and didn't allow him to slow down.

They arrived at the shop without incident but the horse was blowing and sweating when they tied him to a post at the gable to the shop. The three men went inside and gave the shopkeeper their list of required goods.

The shop had a licence to sell alcohol but only for off-sales. However, the shopkeeper had a small room at the rear of the premises, and here he used to sell drink, by the glass, to his friends and trusted customers.

The farmer and his sons settled down to enjoy a drink or two with no thought for the welfare of the horse. The horse was hot, he had no food or water and he was most unhappy. He snorted and stamped his hooves on the ground.

Despite the fact that he had not been unyoked he reared up on his hind legs. When he crashed down his front feet it was on top of a barrel of porter. He stove in the wooden lid and began to drink the stout. By the time the farmer and his sons came out of the shop the horse had drunk the whole eleven gallons in the barrel. Unaware of what had taken place they loaded up the gig, climbed onboard, and set out for home.

After a short distance the horse began to stagger, he was all rubber legged and finally he collapsed, dead to the world. The farmer was distraught, it would be costly to replace such a fine beast and he had the more immediate problem of how they were going to get their messages transported back home.

They walked back to the shop. The shopkeeper expressed his sorrow when he heard that their horse was dead. He was able to help and offered a loan of his horse to take their gig home. The farmer promised they would return the following day, take back the shopkeeper's horse, and bury the dead animal.

The farmer, mean as always, did not like the idea of their horse being a total loss so, before setting out for home, they skinned him. But they had to leave the hide at the shop as they already had too much in the gig to take it with them. The journey back home was a sombre one but they unloaded the gig and the shopkeeper's horse was let loose in a park near the farmhouse.

The next morning the farmer woke to the sound of a horse's hooves on the gravel path at the front of the house. He thought that the shopkeeper's horse had somehow got out of the park. However, when he looked out his bedroom window he saw, to his horror and astonishment, his own skinned horse standing shivering in the cold air of the morning.

# The Woolly Horse

~ ~ ~

He dressed quickly, aroused his sons, and led the poor animal into the stable. They gave him a bucket of warm water and wondered how they could cover him. The housekeeper, hearing all the commotion, arrived on the scene. Without saying anything she began to cover the naked horse with the skins from the slaughtered sheep.

The housekeeper was a very accomplished seamstress and very soon she had the skinned horse neatly covered. They fed him and he seemed surprisingly comfortable. All day they watched the horse, they were sure that he would die; it was unthinkable that he could survive such an awful experience.

As the days passed the horse got better and better, the fine weather continued and the animal was allowed outside. After a few weeks the farmer began to believe that the horse would, indeed, live. He was even more amazed when he noticed that the wool on the horse was growing.

The horse lived for many, many years after that. As well as carting, pulling the plough, harrowing and all the other work that a horse did on a farm, he became the most valuable animal in the parish because he yielded twenty-eight pounds of quality wool each year!

*This story is well known in north Yell and it was first told by the late John Thomas Anderson of Backhouse.*

# 20

## Robbie's Voyage

ROBBIE was a fourteen-year-old boy who lived at Midbrake in north Yell. Many of his older friends had gone to sea to learn to be seamen and travel the world. Robbie longed to do this too. He had a great liking for the sea and he had made a start by spending the summer on a fishing boat. Fishing skippers would, quite often, take on two youths, boys recently left school, to work together, the two of them counting as one man.

In the early years of the 20th century herring around the shores of Shetland were abundant. Every voe, every firth and every anchorage had herring stations – places where herring were landed, gutted and salted in barrels, by crews of women and young girls and boys. The finished product was exported to eastern Europe and further. Continental buyers and traders would come to Shetland to bargain for the salt herring.

Buyers would test the herring before committing themselves to purchase. They would order several barrels to be opened and they would test the quality by taking a bite out of the back of a fish from each barrel. They would then begin the business of agreeing a price.

But it was late September now and the herring fishing season was finished for the year. Robbie was kicking his heels at home waiting, impatiently, for a chance to go to sea. The practice was that when an established seaman came home on leave then he would be asked to take a boy away south with him, under his wing, and find him a job on a ship.

There had been some bad gales. It was the time of year when day and night are of equal length, and strong winds, at this time, are seasonal and expected. One morning Robbie's mother was making tea, as she always did around 11 o'clock. She put the last of the drinking water into the kettle and asked Robbie to go to the well and bring back some more.

In the back porch there were two benches. On one side was a row of water buckets and on the other side was the milk, buttermilk and the big earthenware jar that milk was gathered in for churning. It was a good place to keep milk as the back porch got no sunlight and it was always cool.

Robbie took two buckets and started on his way to the well. The wind had moderated, it was bright and clear but he could still hear the noise of the sea that, even now, had not yet calmed down. The well was at a place called the Hammers and sometimes it dried up in summer. It had water now and Robbie filled up his two buckets.

Robbie's eyes never strayed far from the sea and as he looked out over the Wick of Breckon he saw a white painted sailing ship. As he watched, the ship came closer and closer to the shore and dropped anchor. It was clear that the ship had suffered from the bad weather. The top of the main mast was lying at a crazy angle, the rigging was damaged and some of the sails were in tatters.

A small boat was lowered down and four oarsmen rowed towards the shore. Robbie left the water buckets and hurried to meet the men from the boat. They landed in the geo of Hirpital and Robbie found that they were Norwegian. Their ship, a barque, was called the *Gudrun* and they had experienced a really rough trip across the North Sea. As well as all the damage they had sustained, a man had been lost overboard.

What they needed, and needed badly, was a safe place and a pilot to guide them there so they could repair the damage. Robbie immediately volunteered to be the pilot. He told them about his summer on the fishing boat and that he knew every rock and hazard in the area. He promised to take the *Gudrun* into Cullivoe, a safe anchorage. The Norwegians were unconvinced, they thought that he was far too young, but they agreed to take him to see the ship's captain.

The captain, too, had his doubts about Robbie's worth as a pilot and he closely questioned Robbie about the area.

After a period of consideration the captain said, "Robbie, you are all we have. I am going to take a chance on you, but pity help you if you steer us in to any danger."

The wind was light to moderate from the north-west and therefore helpful. Without any untoward incident they were able to anchor in Cullivoe well before nightfall. The men set to work right away in their task of making the *Gudrun* fully seaworthy again. So intent were they in their work that they appeared to forget all about Robbie.

Robbie became impatient and, at last, he summed up his courage and asked to be put ashore.

"I am sorry, Robbie," said the captain, "but you are going to stay with us. We lost a good man overboard in the North Sea, you have not been with us long but you have shown me enough, I know that I can make a seaman you of you."

Robbie argued and protested but to no avail. When, at last, he accepted his fate and asked where they were going, the captain told him that they were outward bound with a cargo of pit props to Newcastle-Upon-Tyne. The props were for the mining industry.

When the repairs were finished to the captain's satisfaction the *Gudrun* raised anchor and set sail. The wind continued from the north-west, it was now a fresh breeze. They headed south past Fetlar and Whalsay and onward to Newcastle.

Robbie was seriously worried about his parents, he wanted them to know that he was alive and well. However, life was so exciting aboard the *Gudrun* and there was so much to learn that he soon forgot about home. He proved the captain right. He was an apt pupil and soon he was up to nearly every task expected of a seaman. He was light and agile, he had no fear of heights and he could scamper in the rigging like a monkey.

Newcastle was reached safely and with no more bad weather, and work began at once to discharge the cargo. The captain was on the lookout for another cargo to take somewhere else. The *Gudrun* was a tramp ship that delivered merchandise wherever it had to go, anywhere in the world.

At the first opportunity Robbie announced his intention to go back home.

"Do you think that you are doing the right thing?" asked the captain. "You have no way of getting home, Robbie. There is no passenger service between Newcastle and Shetland. Besides, you have no money."

Robbie realised that he was in a fix, how would he get home? He was aware that the captain was speaking again.

"I'll tell you a better idea, why don't you sign on as a seaman on the *Gudrun*? I will give you full pay as a man and I will promise you that, when it is possible, I will take you back to where we picked you up."

It did not take Robbie too long to make up his mind. He really liked the life on the *Gudrun* and going to sea was what he always wanted anyway. His shipmates were easy to get on with and he was eager to see many more strange places, not just Newcastle. He was in for a shock, however, when he asked where they were going next.

"We are going on a long, long voyage," the captain told him. "This very day I have obtained a cargo of coal to be delivered to Valparaiso, a seaport in Chile, on the west coast of South America."

"Does that mean we have to round Cape Horn?" asked Robbie.

Robbie had heard plenty about Cape Horn. He had heard sailor men tell of hardships, adventures and disasters experienced in this notorious part of the southern ocean.

"It does that," the captain confirmed. "No man can ever call himself a seaman until he has rounded the Horn."

As soon as the cargo was loaded and provisions taken on board they set sail for the far south. They sailed down the east coast of England and turned west into the Channel. The captain headed well west before setting a course calculated to pick up the favourable trade winds.

It was a big day when they crossed the equator. Robbie was pleased to find that some of the other crewmembers, like him, had never before crossed the line. Another thing new to Robbie was the fact that they were sailing into the southern summer and the weather was hot. The sun blazed down out of a cloudless sky and any kind of work was an effort.

Day after day they proceeded south. The days ran into weeks and Robbie wondered if the trip would ever end. Not that he was unhappy, every day he learned something new and he loved to spend his spare time sitting at the top of the main mast with the lookout, marvelling at the vastness of the mighty ocean.

The food on board the *Gudrun* was like any sailing ship, plain and rough. The salt meat and salt fish was exactly the fare that he was used to at home. The bread, baked on board by the cook, was much the same too and the hard ship's biscuits were no great challenge to his young strong teeth. However, as fresh food ran out entirely, the diet was a bit monotonous.

There was big excitement all through the ship when the lookout shouted, "Land ho!"

On getting a little closer the land was identified as Staten Island. This meant they were close to the dreaded Cape Horn. The captain was a cautious man and, again, he continued well south before heading west into the head wind, the roaring forties. The wind reached gale force and beyond and these were the worst conditions experienced by the *Gudrun* since that first week in the North Sea.

Sometimes no headway was made at all. The sky had a blanket covering of cloud and it was impossible to get a sighting of the sun. Navigation was, therefore, largely guesswork. So far south the weather became cold despite the summer season and the misery was made worse because men's clothes were wet all the time.

Little by little they edged further and further west until, at last, the captain was sure that it was safe to change course and head north. This made a welcome change. They had been sailing close hauled, tacking through the roaring forties, for five weeks. As the weather improved they sighted the South American continent on the starboard beam.

The Pacific Ocean is never still. The swell was slow but deep, but with favourable wind good progress was made and the crew began to look forward to some time ashore in Valparaiso. As soon as the ship tied up in port the first priority was to unload the cargo of coal.

## Robbie's Voyage

~ ~ ~

The discharging was done under the watchful eye of the chief officer. The captain was ashore negotiating their next assignment.

Late in the afternoon he came back to the *Gudrun* looking very pleased with himself. A shipping agent had a cargo of phosphates that he wanted delivered to Bordeaux in France. Not only that but they need have no waiting time, the cargo was there, ready to be loaded onboard. Robbie found Valparaiso a fascinating place and he was sorry to hear that they were going to put to sea so soon.

In Valparaiso, for the first time in his life, Robbie saw black people and people with skin colours that were very different from his own colour and that of the Norwegians. The language, Spanish, sounded strange, to say nothing of the dialect of the native people.

The trip back to Europe went well. Rounding Cape Horn was no problem this time because the prevailing wind was in their favour. The only delay they had was a brief spell in the doldrums, becalmed, near the equator. The captain declared that this was one of the fastest passages he had ever made from west coast South America to Europe.

In Bordeaux they got a cargo of wine to take to Kingston, Jamaica, in the West Indies. The Caribbean was a very popular destination with all the crew of the *Gudrun*. The wine was for a rich plantation owner who wanted it for himself, his friends and to sell on.

"That is what we signed up for," one of them said. "The sun and the palm trees, the rum and the bananas."

It meant, of course, another trip across the Atlantic and some tricky navigation among the hundreds of islands that make up the West Indies. On arrival at Kingston they found another cargo awaiting them. The owner of the wine had a large order for sugar and rum, his own produce, which was to be delivered to Cape Town in South Africa.

So it was another Atlantic crossing and another crossing of the equator. However, destination was reached without major incident and the cargo was safely unloaded. The captain could not believe his luck. Never before in his experience had work come to him so easily. He was offered a cargo of exotic hardwood and ivory to be delivered to Galveston, in Texas.

The wood they carried was mostly ebony. It, and the ivory, was destined for a large firm of instrument makers. They made pianos and organs; the ivory was for the keys. On arrival in the U.S.A. they had no difficulty in finding yet another cargo. This time a cargo of cotton, for the mills of Lancashire in England. They were homeward bound to Liverpool.

For the first time in many months Robbie felt a bit homesick. He asked the captain if there was any chance of him getting back home again.

"There is," he replied. "We have all been a long time away from home. Believe me, I very much want to see my wife and family again. If I can find a cargo in Liverpool that takes us anywhere near Scandinavia we will all go home. I have not forgotten the promise that I made you in Newcastle."

The entire ship's company was bitterly disappointed when they could find no cargo in Liverpool. They lay idle for ten days before the captain decided that he could wait no longer. He ordered ballast to be loaded and they sailed, light ship, for Newcastle. There was always coal there to be moved around the world.

As luck would have it they got a cargo of coal going to Oslo, just what they wanted. The trip north was full of high spirits and for Robbie the sighting of a Shetland shoreline was a big moment indeed. The captain was as good as his word. He sailed up Yell Sound and anchored in the Wick of Breckon.

The small boat was lowered and Robbie was put ashore in the Geo of Hirpital. It was with very mixed feeling that Robbie said goodbye to the *Gudrun* and his shipmates. He had become one of the crew in every way and wondered if he would ever see any of them again.

As he walked slowly up the hill from the shore he realised that he had been away for exactly three years, to the hour. When he reached the well he was greatly surprised to find his two buckets of water still there. He picked them up and carried them to the house, into the back porch and set the buckets on the bench.

When he came into the kitchen his mother poured him a cup of tea and gave him an oatcake. "You have been a long while away at the well," she said.

## Robbie's Voyage

~ ~ ~

He did not reply, but he was aware that he had, in fact, been away longer than necessary. He had been sitting by the shore daydreaming!

*Robbie was my uncle, my father's oldest brother.*
*He was a great storyteller. He lived in London and*
*he told this on one of his rare visits home.*

# 21

## The Laird's Son

THERE was a dynasty of lairds in Midbrake in north Yell called Irvine. One of them had a son who was a ship's captain. It was said that he was the youngest man ever to be in command of a sailing ship leaving Liverpool. He was only twenty-three years old.

Young Captain Irvine had been well educated and he spoke with an accent unknown in Shetland. He was very fond of using big words to describe even the simplest situation. Another strange thing was that he would not allow any Shetlanders on his ship.

Other ships welcomed Shetlanders as crewmen. Not only were they natural seamen and expert at handling small boats, but also they were, on the whole, placid and willing to take orders. However, Captain Irvine would not have them at any price.

When Captain Irvine's ship was lying in Liverpool one Shetlander did manage to sign on. He disguised his voice – knappit – and he gave the address of the lodging house that he had been staying in while waiting for a ship.

Captain Irvine, being so young, was full of energy. He prowled from stem to stern of the ship and he was very fussy, everything had to be exactly the way he wanted it to be. The Shetlander kept as much as possible out of his way so as to remain undetected.

One day, however, he was standing close to the captain when Irvine noticed that one of the sails was not standing quite right, it was spilling the wind.

# The Laird's Son
~ ~ ~

Looking directly at the Shetlander, he ordered, in a loud voice, "Lie along to the furthest extremity of the lee fore yard and ascertain what detains the lee fore sheet from attaining its destination."

The man did as he was told, but he forgot himself and shouted back in a strong Shetland accent, "Dirs a kale bled ida shaeve hol, sir!"

And that blew his cover good and proper.


Once, when his ship was lying in Bristol, Captain Irvine decided to go ashore and see something of the West Country. He hired a horse and trap and set off inland. The countryside was beautiful, the weather was pleasant, and he was in a land very different from his native Shetland.

So far did he go that he realised he would have to spend the night away from the ship. He found a likely looking inn so he pulled up at the door and shouted for the innkeeper to attend to him and the horse.

With regard to the horse he ordered, "Extricate the quadruped from the vehicle and administer onto him an adequate supply of nutritious element. When the aurora of the morning doth illuminate the oriental horizon, I will reward you a pecuniary recompense for your amiable hospitality."


*I heard the first part of this story from the late Bertie Henderson of West-A-Firth and also from the late Lowry Williamson of Sellafirth. The second part I got from my father.*

# 22

## Long Willie Henderson

WILLIAM Henderson of Gloup, Yell, was, in his time, a local hero. He was a soldier in the Napoleonic wars and serving under the Duke of Wellington he attained the rank of captain. He fought in the Battle of Waterloo but he was wounded – one of his heels was shot off.

He retired to Gloup after that and was obliged to wear a piece of cork in his boot to compensate for his injury. Locals, somewhat unkindly, gave him the nickname Corkheel.

According to legend, Captain Henderson was shown great respect by both Wellington and Napoleon. The story is told that on the morning of the battle, the Duke of Wellington was very uneasy. He was not at all confident of the outcome and was, therefore, reluctant to commence hostilities. He felt that he needed reinforcements. He paced restlessly up and down, unable to make up his mind.

A young aide was in attendance awaiting orders from the great man.

"Have you seen Captain Henderson this morning?" Wellington asked him.

"Yes, sir," replied the young man.

"What was he doing?"

"Please, sir, he was sitting outside his tent drinking tea and smoking his pipe."

"Has he had breakfast?" was the next question.

"Yes, sir, I'm sure he has."

"Do you think that he is ready to fight?"

"Sir, I reckon he's as ready as he can be."

"Rightho," said Wellington, "in that case we'd better begin!"

The battle was joined, and for a long time it was all far too close to call. Napoleon was nervous too. He was seated on his horse on a hillock where he had a good view of events. So anxious was he that he spoke to no one, except to bark essential orders. He was motionless and poker faced.

Towards midday, Captain Henderson led out his company of men, and this was what it took to break Napoleon's reserve. He became very excited and started to jump up and down on his horse.

Such was his panic that for a time the power of speech deserted him and then he began to scream, "There goes Long Willie Henderson from Gloup. Shoot him, boys, shoot him!"

*The first part of this story was told to me by Robert Scollay of Lerwick, who used to live in Sellafirth. The second part I heard from my father many years before that.*

# 23

## Jimmy Hert

JIMMY Hert, or Herty as some would have it, was a man who lived in Gloup, Yell, in the second half of the 19th century. It is hard to imagine anyone as poor or as destitute as he was. He lived in a miserable hovel at the eastern end of the Beach of Whallery. Quite literally, he had nothing except a few rags of clothing, and his pride that did not allow him to beg.

He did not need to beg. He had good kind neighbours who were poor people too, but they were willing to share with him what little they had. If they saw him passing they would call him in and give him a cup of tea, an oatcake, or whatever they had. If it were a mealtime they would invite him to sit in at their table.

If any of the local men went to the fishing they would always call along Jimmy Hert and gave him a diet of fresh fish, but he was a proud man and sometimes he avoided the neighbours because he did not want them to think that he was sponging off them. The end result was that he often went hungry.

As a younger man he had worked at Nethertoon, at the haaf fishing station. For one reason or another he had never been a fisherman, but when the sixtreens came back to the shore he was the tallyman. He kept a record, on behalf of Mr Pole who owned the boats, of the amount of fish landed.

Nethertoon was a very big fishing station and it was near to where Jimmy Hert lived. He had always been a poor man but while he was working at the beach at least fish was plentiful.

# Jimmy Hert

~ ~ ~

The fish caught was mostly ling, big fish that were split and had the backbone taken out, then salted and dried for export. Herty knew all about poverty. Especially poor were the widows and their families. Accidents at sea happened all too often and there were no welfare services to take care of the needy.

Merchants like Pole were not, as a rule, generous men. If he caught workers like Jimmy Hert giving away fish to the poor, Pole could be very angry indeed. To get around this the beach boys would be told by Jimmy Hert to make a poor job of the filleting. They would leave a lot of the fish still attached to the backbone and when these bones were boiled it made a decent meal to those who had nothing else.

The disaster of July 1881 was virtually the end of the haaf fishing from Gloup. Six boats and thirty-six men were lost in a severe storm that caught the fishermen unawares. It was a tragedy that affected the lives of every family in north Yell. Not only were widows and orphans left without breadwinners but some of the owners tried to sue them to recover the cost of the boats that their husbands and fathers were lost in. Some of the lairds even went so far as to visit bereaved families and take from them anything they had of value as part payment.

For Jimmy Hert this all meant he no longer had a job and this was why, in his later years, he was so very poor. He was also a simple man who was ill-equipped for earning money or looking after himself.

In the late 1890s, Andrina Tulloch was a young married woman who lived with her family in the Haa of Midbrake. One day, when she was bringing home peats for the fire, she heard the terrible sounds of a man weeping and crying. At first she could not see where the sound was coming from but she went towards the source.

She found Jimmy Hert sitting in a deep drain beside the road. He was in a dreadful state, sobbing and gasping and incoherent. It took Andrina some time to calm him down and find out what had happened.

He had been without food for two days. There was no morsel whatsoever in his house so he had walked the two miles or so to the Greenbank shop. When he got there, Joseph Pole, the shopkeeper, would give him nothing. He showed Jimmy Hert his ledger. Jimmy Hert owed him money. Pole told him angrily that until he paid his debt he could have nothing, and he ordered him out of his shop.

Such was Herty's desperation and hunger that he did something he had never done before in his life; with the tears running into his beard he went down on his knees and begged.

"One pound of meal, please, Mr Pole, please give me one pound of meal."

Pole dragged him to his feet, shoved him outside, and shut the door. Herty had no option but to trudge homewards. When he got to the place where Andrina Tulloch found him he could go no further, he was in a state of collapse.

When he recovered somewhat she took him into the house and made him tea and gave him biscuits and oatcakes to eat. Before he left Midbrake she went into the meal chest and filled a small bag with oatmeal for him to take home. He blessed her and cursed Pole but his distress was eased, at least for a few days.

But his problems did not end there. In the great gale of February 1900 his house was all but washed away. When one of his neighbours, Robbie Henderson, saw the sea breaking over the roof of Jimmy Hert's house he went to rescue him.

Normally it would only take a few minutes to walk the length of the beach, but on that day the sea was so heavy that Robbie had to take a very long way around to get to the other end. When he got there he could not open the door. Needless to say the door was not locked, Jimmy Hert did not have such a thing, but when he did get in he found a large cod behind the door.

Every time he told this story Robbie said that the cod had come down the chimney with the heavy sea. In fact, the fish had been washed out of a store at the back, where salt fish were stored.

Jimmy Hert was rescued but he was never back in his own house again, he ended his days in comfort living with the Henderson family.

*I have pieced this story together from a number of sources, firstly from my father and from Andrew and the late Danny Anderson of Midfield, Cullivoe. Sadly, the story is true; Andrina Tulloch was my grandmother.*

# 24

## Heatherdale

IN THE second half of the 19th century the most powerful and wealthiest merchant in north Yell was Joseph Pole. He owned a number of sixtreens, the open boats that went far out to the haaf fishing, and he owned two shops. One shop was at Greenbank in Cullivoe and the other was in Heatherdale.

The old name for Heatherdale is Glippapund and it was a most unlikely location for a business. It is in the valley at the head of Gloup voe, the valley that goes most of the way to Bastavoe. It is a very beautiful place, sheltered and isolated, with hardly any houses nearby.

The ruins of the shop are still there to be seen. It had been a stone built house and shop with freestone around the doors and windows. Heatherdale never had a road to it; it is surrounded by magnificent wilderness. Everything for sale in the shop had to be carried there from Cullivoe where the pier was situated.

One of Mr Pole's few neighbours was a man called Thomas Moar, a man with an extremely strong back and a weak mind. He was more commonly known as Tammie Toilky and Pole used him as a beast of burden. If anything was needed at the shop then Tammie was sent to fetch it.

Pole owned some of the sixtreens that fished out of Nethertoon, situated near the mouth of Gloup voe. The fishermen were Pole's customers. Many of them lived in the Dalsetter and

Sellafirth area and they would walk past Heatherdale on their way to and from the fishing station.

Pole was not one who liked anything to be wasted so he was in the habit of keeping a pig at Nethertoon. The pig was fed the scraps from the fish curing. Ling, cod and other fish was filleted, salted and dried for the export market. The pig had little else to eat but it seemed to be enough.

One year the fishing finished prematurely because of unseasonable weather and the pig was not nearly fat enough to kill. Of course, there was no more food at Nethertoon, so it had to be taken to Heatherdale. Needless to say it was Tammie Toilky who had to do the fetching.

Pigs are likeable and intelligent animals but they are impossible to reason with and it is impossible to either lead or drive them. In this regard poor Tammie Toilky was on a steep learning curve and it was no time at all until his patience with the pig was exhausted.

He turned the pig on to its back and tied its legs, swung the pig on his neck, and carried it the same way as a shepherd may carry a lamb. He then set off to walk out the Leas of Gloup, the three miles to Heatherdale.

The Leas of Gloup are very steep, it is the nearest thing to a Norwegian fjord in Shetland. The path is narrow, little more than a sheep gaet; a hazardous walk at the best of times but carrying a heavy, struggling pig it was almost suicidal. Nor was the pig very happy. So loudly did it scream and reehan in Tammie's ear that he was deaf for the next three days!

Pole ordered crockery from the wholesalers to resell in the shop and again he sent Tammie Toilky to fetch it from the steamer that came to the pier at Cullivoe. The dishes came well packed in a heavy wooden chest and Tammie had to carry it all the way to Heatherdale through the hill and without even a path to follow.

Pole was a hard unfeeling man who had to be obeyed and served. He had the power to evict any individual or family unwise enough to cross him or unlucky enough to be in his bad books. A poor man like Tammie Moar had no option but to do exactly as he was told.

# Heatherdale

~ ~ ~

Another resident of north Yell at that time was Charles Fraser of Midbrake. He was a tenant and a crofter but far more importantly he was recognised as a master builder and carpenter. He could trace his ancestry back to the Frasers, the master masons who were brought to Shetland in the 1590s to help build the Castle of Muness in Unst.

Although he seldom went to sea Fraser was an expert on boats. Whenever a new fishing boat came to north Yell, the owners always consulted him and sought his opinion. If he suggested any alterations to the boat then his advice was always taken.

He did not build boats but he spent much of his time working on them. If a vessel needed repairs he would be the man to do the job. Because of this Fraser had quite a lot of dealings with Pole. Pole had his fleet of boats at Gloup and, in the course of a fishing season, the boats required certain maintenance.

One autumn Pole bargained to buy a colt foal from Fraser. Pole got the foal but he would pay for it when he was good and ready and at no other time. Fraser was eventually summonsed to get his money; the price agreed was four sovereigns, a handsome sum in those days.

By this time it was winter and the ground was covered by a fall of fresh snow. It was evening when Fraser set out to walk to Heatherdale; a beautiful evening with a clear sky, a full moon and severe frost. As he left home he walked through his own back yard and down the Whilks, across the voot and through the hill grind.

The snow in Litealater and on the Hill of Midbrake was untrodden by the human foot, the only marks to be seen were the paths of sheep and rabbits. Charles went through Klody, the peat cutting area, and on to the Gill of Sandwater before reaching the top of the Easter Lea of Gloup voe.

From there it was a short but tricky walk down into Heatherdale and to Pole's house. Fraser was well received by Pole. He was given some refreshment and paid the money due to him, four sparkling gold coins in mint condition. It was with a light step and a feeling of the utmost satisfaction that Fraser returned home keen to show this bonanza to his family.

However, by the time he reached Midbrake it was late and he was tired; walking a long distance through deep snow takes its toll.

His wife, Margaret, had stayed up to wait for his return so, triumphantly, he went into his pocket to show her the gold coins. His dismay was total when he could only find three of them.

He knew which pocket he had put them in. Nonetheless, he went through all his pockets but in vain. On close inspection he discovered a hole in his trouser pocket, a hole big enough that a small coin like a sovereign could slip through. He knew then that he had lost it.

This represented a huge loss. It turned, in an instant, his triumph into despair. Late as it was, and tired as he was, he retraced his steps back towards Heatherdale, hoping against hope that he would find the lost coin. The moon made the light as bright as day and there were no tracks to be seen bar his own.

He was determined to go all the way, even as far as Heatherdale itself, but his eyes lit up when he reached the boundary fence above the Lea of Gloup. His gaze was drawn to an object glinting in the moonlight. As he had crossed the fence earlier a lump of snow had fallen from his boot, sticking in it, on its edge, was his precious sovereign.

*This is another of my father's stories, I heard him tell this many times.*

# 25

## Canvas Jackets

WHENEVER sailor men meet they always tell each other of the epic voyages they have made to exotic parts of the world. One-upmanship is the order of the day and it is far from unknown for some to stretch and maximize the hardships and the heroics they experienced.

The men who were at sea during the time of sailing ships had very hard times and their occupation was hazardous in the extreme. One windjammer man was heard to say that he was going to give up being a seaman altogether and sign on a steamer!

Two sailors were having a yarn about their days at sea and one of them was telling the story of the time that they were becalmed off the west coast of Africa. This was the notorious Skeleton Coast that had claimed the lives of hundreds of seafarers. Ashore is desert so, even if shipwreck itself is overcome, survival is extremely unlikely.

There are hundreds of miles of sandbanks and for any ship to run aground there is fatal. Therefore, to be in a situation where you are drifting closer and closer to the shore without a breath of wind to sail your ship is perilous indeed. They had every sail that they could find set, in the hope of taking advantage of any cat's-paw of wind.

In desperation the captain ordered boats to be lowered and men took turns at the oars in the hope of towing the ship away from this treacherous shore. The ship had been at sea for a long time and her bottom was badly fouled by barnacles and weeds. The sun was burning hot and no progress whatsoever was made.

One day around noon, the lookout at the masthead shouted an urgent warning. A black cloud had suddenly appeared, it indicated a severe squall and the officer of the watch called for all hands to go aloft and shorten sail. Such was this new danger that he told seamen that if they did not have time to take down a sail they were to rip it with their knives so that it could not catch the wind and tear out the masts.

The men responded as best they could but they were far too late, the cloud was upon them with lighting speed. However, to their amazement there was no wind, the threatening cloud was not a tropical storm but, in fact, a swarm of locusts. The men could only stand and watch while the insects ate every stitch of canvas from the masts. When they flew on they left nothing but bare poles.

The other seaman listened carefully to this story and asked quite a lot of questions. He wanted to know when this happened and the exact position of the ship at the time.

He sat silent, deep in thought, before he spoke again. "My ship," he said, "was in that area at the same time but we were further out to sea, and I reckon we saw the same plague of locusts because when they landed on our masts we could see that each and every one of them was wearing a canvas jacket!"

*I heard this story from the late John Anderson who used to live in North House in Gutcher. John was a great yarner and I spent many happy hours in his company.*

# 26

## The Sheep Thief of Easterhouse

IN SHETLAND people have nicknames depending on which island or parish they live in. It is a bit like the way that folk from Liverpool are called Scousers and folk from Newcastle are called Geordies. The people from the island of Yell are called Sheep Thieves.

It could be that it came about because of the activities of William Jamieson who lived in Easterhouse, Gloup. He stole sheep on a regular basis and got away with it for a long time until his wife informed on him. After that the ranselmen kept a close watch on him.

The ranselmen were the forerunners of the police service. They were responsible for law and order and they regarded sheep stealing as a very serious crime indeed. The reason Mrs Jamieson informed on her husband was because she did not want him anymore. She was having a love affair with the man next door.

Jamieson did his sheep stealing on Sundays. He chose Sundays because almost everyone went to the kirk and that left him in Gloup all by himself. Of course, this made his crime even worse because the kirk and the ranselmen demanded total Sabbath observance; all work, even of an honest nature, was strictly forbidden.

If all this was not bad enough it was from the Laird of Midbrake that he stole, and one Sunday he had taken another man's dog to help him catch the sheep. Jamieson had killed a sheep and was in the act of skinning it when he saw the ranselmen approaching the house.

He was working in the butt end and his wife was lying in a box bed that they had in the room. Mrs Jamieson spent a lot of time in bed. She always complained of feeling ill so that she avoided work and avoided helping her husband in any way.

Jamieson immediately looked for some way of hiding the evidence. He had little time, so what he did was put the dead sheep, along with the severed head and legs, into the bed beside his wife and cover it with the blankets. The ranselmen forced their way into the house, accused Jamieson of sheep stealing, and announced their intention of searching the house.

They found nothing, and there was no question of them violating a woman's bed. However, when Jamieson was not looking, Mrs Jamieson caught the eye of one of the searchers and slightly lifted the covers so that the sheep was discovered. And that was how William Jamieson was caught and sent for trial.

It came as no surprise when he was found guilty, and his wife would have been well aware that his punishment would be severe.

His sentence came in several parts. First of all he was banished for life from Yell, and he had the lobes of both ears cut off to mark him, for all time, as a thief. Last, but not least, he was appointed deemster at the Court of Lerwick and this meant, among other things, that he was the hangman.

*I heard this story from my father but the court records tell something of William Jamieson, the Sheep Thief of Easterhouse.*

# 27

## The Polar Bear

THE whaling industry in the Arctic flourished during the 19th century. Whaling ships from ports like Dundee, Whitby and Hull used to call at Lerwick to pick up extra crew. The ships would have enough men on board to sail them but they needed more for the actual catching of whales.

The harpooning of whales was extremely dangerous work and it called for considerable expertise in the handling of small boats. This was where the Shetlanders came in. They were experienced with small boats and they were strong rowers, making them ideal for the job.

One whaling ship had a really poor season; they caught very few whales. The captain, therefore, ventured further north than usual and they stayed on beyond the normal whaling season. The end result was that they got frozen-in in a bay at the north of Greenland. Try as they might they could not break free of the pack ice and they were faced with the prospect of over-wintering in Greenland.

It was a Scots ship and, of course, Scotsmen and Shetlanders did not mix very well, so the Shetlanders decided that they would leave the ship and spend the winter in a trapper's hut on the beach. The big concern was to find enough food to keep them alive until spring.

They hunted seals. Seals were plentiful and the extreme cold kept any meat fresh. However, they wanted some variety in their diet but this was near impossible. The only other eatable animals near them were polar bears but they were such big, fierce and formidable brutes that no one wanted to cross them.

One of the Shetlanders, an eighteen-year-old called Willie, making his first trip to the whaling, volunteered to go and shoot a bear. The only firearm they had was an old muzzle-loading shotgun but they loaded it up with some extra gunpowder and plenty of shot. Willie set out, fearlessly, on his quest.

He had only gone a short distance when he rounded a headland and there, came face to face with an enormous male bear that reared up to be almost twice as tall as Willie. Putting the gun to his shoulder, but without taking any careful aim, Willie pulled the trigger. This did the bear no physical damage but it made it awful mad.

Of course, there was no time to reload and Willie turned tail and ran as fast as he could back towards the hut. Even Willie's top speed was no match for the bear and it was getting closer with every bound. So close was the bear that Willie could feel its breath on the back of his neck.

Another few strides and the bear would have caught him, but Willie tripped over a stone and fell flat on his face. By this time they were very near the hut. The bear was going flat out too and could not get stopped; it struck the door of the hut, smashed it open and disappeared inside among the rest of the men.

Willie had his pride. He did not want the older men to think the bear had chased him so, quick as a flash, he got to his feet and shouted above the melee, "OK, boys, you flay dis bugger while I go an get anither een."

# The Polar Bear

~ ~ ~

*The first time I heard this story it was told as a joke at a concert staged by pupils from the Anderson High School, in the Mid Yell Hall. This would have been in the 1960s. Later I saw it as a visual sketch on TV.*

# 28

## The Reverend's Ruin

THOMAS Irvine Esquire, the Laird of Midbrake in north Yell, was a truly contented and comfortable man. He was monarch of all he surveyed and his income from his tenants and various business dealings assured him of an adequate lifestyle.

True, he had lost his dear wife Maud, who had died of a fever four years before. However, he had put his grief well behind him. He revelled in the situation where no one challenged his authority or tried to tell him what to do.

His daughter Mary had married well. She was married to a prosperous merchant and they lived just the right distance away. They were within reach if he needed them and far enough away that they gave him no hassle.

Of his son, James, he was immensely proud. James was a sea captain and the youngest captain ever to take a sailing ship out of Liverpool. He was only twenty-three when he was given his first command. Still quite young, he had been to places as far away as Australia, China and South America.

On one of his rare visits home to Shetland, James gave his father a parrot. Mr Irvine doted on the bird and carried it in its cage from room to room. The parrot was his constant companion. During its time at sea the parrot had, unfortunately, picked up a few forecastle words so he could be a bit embarrassing at times. Whenever the parrot spoke out of turn the laird used to laugh indulgently and declare that every one of his tenants would pay twice the rent that he asked for if they could get a glimpse of the parrot.

Life, reflected the laird, had never been so good. It was wintertime now and he looked back at the autumn with a glow of the utmost satisfaction. A Dutch ship had called at Cullivoe. The captain had bought all the salt fish that Mr Irvine had in store. Not only that, but he had paid quite a lot more than the going rate. Mr Irvine had in turn bought from the Dutchman thirty barrels of salt and enough wood to build a new sixteen to add to his fishing fleet.

As a perk, and to seal the bargain, Captain Kees Kok had given the laird a large pig of gin, enough for his Yule dram and enough that he could have a nightcap every evening during the winter. Such was his current prosperity that he had employed another servant to be at his beck and call.

As he sat by the fire he planned the future. He had a round of social engagements to fulfil. Every winter he invited the minister and his wife to spend an evening with him. Never one to let the grass grow under his feet he, then and there, wrote an invitation and sent a servant to deliver it.

At the manse the invitation received a mixed reception. The Rev John Oliphant enjoyed the laird's company; he liked the rough good humour and the worldliness that came from a different background to his own. Mrs Oliphant regarded the laird as coarse and vulgar and, as for the parrot, she could only push her lips together in a straight line and shake her head.

On the night of the visit Mrs Oliphant, not unexpectedly, developed a severe headache and she declared herself unfit to go to the Haa. She would go to bed early, she said. Mr Oliphant made all the correct noises; he even risked offering to stay home too.

He was, of course, delighted to be going alone. It meant, among other things, that if he were offered a dram he would be able to take it. He had heard about the pig of gin. Outside the night was dry but overcast, there was little wind and it was very dark. Mr Oliphant put a new candle in his lantern, lit it, and set out for the Haa.

The laird greeted his friend with gusto and very soon had him seated in a large comfortable armchair beside the fire. Mr Irvine expressed his deep disappointment on hearing of Mrs Oliphant's indisposition but quickly produced the pig of gin and poured a more than generous measure for each of them. Politeness and status demanded that the minister make a token protest about the size of the dram.

The gin was toothsome, to say the least, and as the glasses were refilled the protests diminished. The laird also provided a bountiful supper washed down by yet another noggin of Dutch gin. For Mr Oliphant the time for going home came all too soon.

The sky had cleared and the moon was shining, as bright as day, on a clear lift. The minister neither noticed nor cared. The length of the road did not trouble him at all but did seem very narrow and he experienced considerable difficulty staying on it. In fact, he found himself in the ditch several times. He was at a loss to understand how he got there, but he felt no pain and he got himself back on the straight and narrow.

It did cross his mind that perhaps his dear wife might accuse him of taking strong drink. With the logic and confidence of the inebriated he laughed out loud and dismissed the thought from his head. He recalled that once, when he was passing a public house, he overheard two men discussing the state of drunkenness. They were agreed that no man could ever be called drunk unless he was obliged to lie on his back and hold on to the grass. Mrs Oliphant, he was certain, would never notice a thing.

Mr Oliphant could not recall going to bed but when he woke up it was broad daylight. The first thing he noticed was that the light from the window was far too bright for his eyes, so he quickly shut them again. He had a headache that would keep his wife away from the Haa for years and years.

But she was up and about and, if he was any judge, her humour was not at all good. He heard her feet in the stairs and a swish and a rustle of skirts and petticoats. When she entered the bedroom it was abundantly clear to even the bleariest of glances that she had a full head of steam and it was close to coming out her ears.

"I," she said, in her frostiest voice, "have put that unspeakable creature out into the porch."

Mr Oliphant had no idea what she was speaking about and to ask was far too risky a strategy. Before he could frame any kind of a reply she was gone again because someone was knocking at the door. All that he could hear was a murmur of low voices and then the familiar swish of skirts announced that her return to the bedroom was imminent.

She came through the door like a middle-aged hen going before a force 12 hurricane. "It's a letter from Mr Irvine," she said, and threw an envelope on the bed.

With a hand that was far from steady, Mr Oliphant broke the seal and withdrew the letter. The writing was indeed the laird's careful copperplate and the letter observed all the niceties of polite correspondence.

It began with "I beg to write" and it finished with "Your Obedient Servant". However, the important bit in the middle was blunt and to the point. It said that, if and when Mr Oliphant returned the laird's parrot, along with the cage, then he could get back his lantern!

*There were lairds in Midbrake by the name of Irvine but this story is largely my own invention.*

# 29

## Life on the *Springbank*

ALL my life I have been close to a framed picture of a sailing ship called the *Springbank*. I remember seeing it first when I was so small that I was sleeping in the same bedroom as my parents. Later, and in another house, it hung on the wall of my bedroom. In our present home it hangs in a place where I see it every day.

My father told me that his uncle, my grand uncle, Nicky Tulloch, was a seaman on the *Springbank*.

Nicky was born at Houlland, Cullivoe, Yell in April 1881. It seems that, as a youth, he got up to more than his fair share of pranks and mischief.

At school the teacher, Mr Clubb, blamed him for each and every prank played. Later, on being told that Nicky had gone away to sea, Mr Clubb caustically declared, "The place will be none the worse without him."

Nicky was a fiddle player and whenever he was home he would be in demand to play at gatherings. In the spring of 1908 he was home and playing at a wedding held at Greenbank in Cullivoe. The dance was in the store of the shop which had been cleared out for the occasion. Nicky's stage was the kirn. He sat on it, in a somewhat precarious position, playing for the dancers.

At weddings in those days it was highly important to give the fiddler the correct amount of drink. Too little and you did not get the best out of him, too much and he got too drunk to play. Indeed, a certain tune was used as a test piece, it had lots of shivers and triplets in it and if the fiddler missed out any of them he had had too much drink and was given no more until he got all the shivers back again.

On this occasion they either did not know about the tune with the shivers, or else they misjudged the quality of playing. In any event, Nicky fell off the kirn and that was the last of his fiddling for the night. There was no other fiddler in the company but Maggie Henderson stepped into the breech and lilted music for the dancers.

The fiddle Nicky was playing that evening has an interesting story. The fiddle was left lying on a chair and the merchant, Denel Sinclair, sat down on it and crushed the belly of it very badly. He had no means of fixing it but to make good the damage he bought the fiddle from Nicky. In time, he got it repaired and put it in his shop for sale. Mrs Thomasina Anderson bought it for her son Jim, but he never learned to play. His much younger brother, Ian, became an excellent fiddler.

Jim Anderson was killed in World War Two and the fiddle became Ian's property. Ian spent much of his life away from Yell but when he left for good he gave Nicky's fiddle to Danny Jamieson. When Danny left Yell he passed it on to Christopher Thomason. Christopher is an appropriate custodian because he is related both to Nicky Tulloch and Ian Anderson.

Nicky Tulloch made many trips to America and once jumped ship in San Francisco. With a partner he worked in the timber industry, but their hut, on a hill overlooking the city, was capsized by the great earthquake of 1906. Fortunately the door was uppermost and they were able to climb out, unhurt, to witness the destruction of San Francisco.

Much later in life his name became, and is to this day, synonymous with sailorly prowess. Once, when a more modern seaman came home 'knappin' after a short time away, a local wag dryly remarked that, "Nicky was sometimes longer on da wan teck as he's been away."

Uncle Nicky told my father of a terrible trip they had made to California in the year 1908. Shortly after the wedding, Nicky went back to sea. With him was another Yell man, Tammy Irvine, who was born in Cunnister in 1890. He, too, was a career seaman, a hard case who made so many trips to west coast America that he was known as Cape Horn Tom or Yankee Tom. He made his home in Leith and finished his working life on the dock gates.

The *Springbank* herself was a four-masted steel barque built by Russell's of Port Glasgow in 1894. So many similar ships were produced that they were known as sausage ships. According to some they were made by the mile and cut off in lengths to be shaped at both ends!

The *Springbank* was 2398 tons, 282.2 feet long, 43 feet beam and had a depth of 24.4 feet. She was owned by Andrew Weir & Co. and used to carry general cargo. She had short top gallant masts known as a jubilee rig, a rig that became popular in the late 1870s.

Nicky Tulloch and Tammy Irvine joined the *Springbank* in Hamburg, Germany. No doubt they knew some of their shipmates because, with the exception of one man from Leith, the Northern Isles provided all the seamen. Some were from Shetland but most were Orcadians. Other Shetlanders included James Hardy and Laurence Tait from Aithsting.

Laurence Tait was only nineteen when he joined the *Springbank*. Ever after his friends knew him as 'Springbank Lowrie'. He was greatly troubled by seasickness and vowed to give up the sea entirely until an older shipmate advised him to buy a pipe and some strong twist tobacco and begin to smoke. Lowrie was never sick again and he continued as a seaman for the rest of his working life.

The master of the *Springbank* was Captain David Royal from Newfoundland. He was 33 years old and a very capable seaman, well liked and respected by all who sailed with him. On this trip, for the first time, he took his wife to sea with him. In five years of marriage they had spent a total of eight months together. To keep the record straight Hannah Royal was signed on as crew and given the rank of stewardess.

The *Springbank* had three mates, six apprentices, a boatswain, a carpenter, a donkeyman, a cook and a steward. Abs and ordinary seamen numbered twenty, making a total ship's company of around forty. In addition to the humans on board there was a goat for milk and a pig called Denis.

# Life on the *Springbank*

~ ~ ~

Things began to go wrong even while they were still in port. Joseph Stenhouse, the 3rd mate became ill. He was diagnosed as having pneumonia and he had to plead with Captain Royal, who wanted to put him ashore. In the end he was allowed to remain. Maybe the fact that he was the son of one of the company directors had something to do with it.

It was at the beginning of June that they set sail, outward bound for Santa Rosalia in Lower California, with a cargo of coke and patient fuels. The cargo was for the copper smelting plant and large ships from many different countries found employment feeding this ever-hungry furnace.

As soon as they reached open sea they ran into bad weather and to everyone's dismay they found that the fully laden *Springbank* handled very badly. She was sluggish, bad to steer, and near impossible to tack. The reason for this was not hard to find. The Plimsoll line had been altered; it was now much higher on her hull.

Samuel Plimsoll had successfully campaigned for a mark to be placed on ships' hulls to ensure that they were never dangerously overloaded. However, the owners of the *Springbank* had applied to the Board of Trade to have the Plimsoll line on their vessel altered on the grounds that the line, as it was, left too great a safety margin. They had won their appeal and the end result was that the *Springbank* was deeper in the water than she had ever been before, hence the poor performance.

As best they could, they made their way westwards through the Fair Isle channel. During this time of rough weather Mrs Royal suffered very badly from seasickness and she spent much of her time confined to bed. However, working their way southwards and into the trade winds saw conditions improve greatly.

Hannah Royal recovered her health and spirits and she took it upon herself to nurse Joseph Stenhouse. She gave him plenty of goat's milk and such medicine as the captain's chest had to offer. Before too long he was back at work. Youth (he was still in his early twenties), along with the warmer weather, restored him to full health and strength.

Seamen on board a square-rigged 'lime juicer' never had an easy time, but when the winds were favourable life was bearable.

Watches below were seldom disturbed and adjustments to the sails were all that was needed. A ship like the *Springbank* could reach a top speed of about 16 or 17 knots. The strength of wind needed to attain this speed would quickly set up a heavy sea and sails would have to be shortened and taken in.

Seamen were always kept busy. As well as the work aloft, scrubbing, cleaning and painting were all daily tasks, as was reeving new ropes. The tradesmen were always busy too; the donkeyman overhauled and greased winches and capstans; the sailmaker always had repairs to do, and caulking was an on-going job with the carpenter.

The Merchant Shipping Act 1906 laid down statutes for the feeding of seamen. If a ship left a home trade port between the end of September and the first of May the owners were obliged to provide enough potatoes for eight weeks. Soft bread (bread baked on board by the cook) had to be served every other day. Coffee mixed with chicory could be used but it had to be 75 per cent coffee.

Fish, too, had to be part of the diet, whether fresh, salted or canned. Also carried by statute were dried vegetables, split peas, haricot beans, flour, rice, oatmeal, tea, sugar, condensed milk, butter, jam, suet, pickles, dried fruit, fine salt, mustard, pepper, curry powder, onions, and, of course, lemon and lime juice. Seamen were entitled to one gallon of water per day.

Allowances were made, under the act, for things going wrong. For example, during bad weather it might not be possible for the cook to light a fire. The preserving of food was not an exact science and sometimes cans of corned beef or salmon were found to be inedible, so substitutions were allowed.

One and a half pounds of fresh meat, a pound of salt meat and three quarters of a pound of canned were all considered equal. Half an ounce of coffee or cocoa and a quarter of an ounce of tea were considered equal. Likewise, a pound of flour, rice or biscuits were considered equal. Half a pint of split peas, three quarters of a pound of flour, half a pint of haricot beans and three quarters of a pound of rice were considered equal when served with meat.

A pound of marmalade or jam and half a pound of butter were considered equal and mustard and curry powder were considered equal. When stocking up with food in the southern hemisphere, where not all European foods were available, equivalents were allowed such as yams for potatoes.

With fine weather cooking was possible and the German cook could serve hot meals. Breakfast was usually porridge and molasses, bugroo as the sailor called it. Molasses featured prominently in the diet and it was much despised. No wonder! It was a thick, black treacle-like substance derived from the residue left in the holds and bilges of sugar carrying ships.

Just as prominent in the diet were ship's biscuits. Put in a canvas bag and pounded to a dust with a belaying pin they offered a variation from the mouth crippling experience of trying to bite them. Biscuit dust mixed with molasses was called dandyfunk; mixed with marmalade or jam, too thin to stay on a whole biscuit, it was called crackerhash. Salt pork, salt beef or salt mutton, collectively known as salt horse, was the staple diet.

As well as the hard life the pay was poor. At that time, 1908, it was £2.10/- per month. As well as their sailorly duties crews were required to work cargo and ballast. Discipline was severe too. Every offence was punished by a fine of five shillings: they included – in the Articles of Agreement – striking any other member of the ship's company; bringing liquor on board; drunkenness; and keeping possession of any firearm, bowie knife, knuckle duster, loaded cane, sword stick or dagger.

Insolent or contemptuous language to the master or any officer, if not otherwise dealt with, usually meant a severe beating and kicking from the fists and boots of a bullying mate. Any seaman caught in the forecastle during his watch was also fined five shillings.

It was, perhaps, in matters of health and safety that sailors were worst off. Accidents were commonplace and many suffered from salt-water boils. Captains were accredited with a certain amount of medical knowledge and each ship had a copy of a book entitled the *Shipmasters Medical Guide*. In the event of surgery the unfortunate patient had to be overpowered by as many of his shipmates as it took while the captain did what he could with the knife. Mrs Royal showed great concern for the plight of the sailors and did whatever she could in the way of nursing.

After crossing the equator the *Springbank* made good progress through the south-east trade winds but the progress was halted when the wind fell to a light air from the south. When, at last, they reached the mouth of the River Plate the wind changed again. It became really nasty with northerly gales and huge seas that became worse and worse.

Lifelines had to be run fore and aft and sails had to be taken in or shortened. Trying to reef a hard blown sail in the pitch dark was extremely dangerous work and sometimes impossible. Standing on a footrope, a hundred feet or more above the deck of a wildly rolling and yawing ship, clinging to the yard with one numbed hand, was a terrible ordeal. Sometimes the only way to shorten sail was with a knife. A quick slash, unseen by the officer of the watch, could reduce a sail to ribbons making more work for the old Montenegrin sail maker.

It was at this time that William Leslie, one of the Orcadian seamen, became ill. A thin man at the best of times, he could not eat and he rapidly lost weight. He had a dry racking cough. The mate and the boatswain needed no convincing that he was really ill. Leslie was a good willing worker and when he could not take his trick at the wheel they knew that his indisposition was nothing trivial.

The weather became colder by the day and there was no let up in the gales. Mrs Royal was seen less and less on deck and Leslie's condition showed no improvement. Worse still, no one knew what was wrong with him, and this left the captain with a very hard decision to make.

He had no way of knowing if the illness was infectious. They did have a place where Leslie could be isolated, a cold, damp, miserable hole under the forecastle head known as the 'hospital'. Leslie was so reluctant to go there that Captain Royal agreed to allow him to stay where he was. While the forecastle was not a very comfortable place for a sick man at least he had the company of his shipmates.

Eighty-two days out of Hamburg, and under no sail save a lower topsail, they sighted Staten Island on the starboard bow. They knew, therefore, that they were in the vicinity of Cosy Corner, as the seamen colloquially called Cape Horn. Cosy it was not. Cape Horn was notoriously difficult to round. Westerly is the prevailing wind and in the latitudes south of South America it is the only place on earth where winds can blow all the way around the world without interruption from any land mass.

Square-riggers could take weeks, even months, to get far enough west to allow a change of course. Thousands were lost in the attempt. The trade from Europe to the west coast was extremely lucrative. Ships took outward-bound coal, and homeward bound phosphates, nitrates and guano. Owners with ships deep laden both ways around Cape Horn became fabulously rich men.

Of course, ships were lost all the way along the trade route, but Cape Horn was, by far, the most hazardous part of the voyage. Official figures showed that in a twenty year period between 1885 and 1905, 4,000 ships and 31,000 men were lost. Of those ships, 1,071 were lost in a single week, in October 1886.

It was little wonder that men deserted en masse from the ships that made it to port. Some 27,000 men jumped ship each year, many of them falling victims of the 'crimping' gangs who sold them back to ship's captains as virtual slaves, for about 15 dollars per man.

With the wind backing into the west the *Springbank* stood well south to make sure that they had plenty of sea room. When they altered course to sail west it was into the teeth of a westerly gale. If life on board was bad before, it was ten times worse now that they were close hauled. The lee rail was constantly buried and the green seas breaking on the forecastle head left hardly any part of the ship dry.

The men were wet all the time and there was nowhere to dry clothes. They had no hot food either. The galley was awash all the time and sometimes the cook was knee deep in saltwater. Any fire that he lit was put out by the next wave that crashed on board.

The lookout on the fore head could not venture from the deckhouse and sometimes it was impossible to relieve him. To walk the length of the ship was a difficult and dangerous undertaking. A slip of a foot, or the failure of frozen hands to cling on to the lifeline, could result in a plummet down the steeply sloping deck to finish bruised, bleeding and half drowned, in the lee scuppers.

# The Foy and other folk tales

~ ~ ~

The weather became so cold that the salt spray froze in the rigging and the running gear would get jammed with ice. Seamen had to use belaying pins to free the blocks. One helmsman could not manage the wheel on his own. Casks were fixed on the deck, on either side of the wheel, so that the two men steering could stand in them free from the very real danger of being washed away.

All hands were needed for most of the time and on one especially bad day some men were aloft continuously for nine hours. The only cheer came with the shout of "grog ho" and each man was given a noggin of gin. Sometimes the seas crashing on the weather bow were so huge that they would lift and slew the *Springbank,* leaving her wallowing in the trough with decks awash.

On more than one occasion they were dismasted and on more than one occasion they were compelled to turn and run before the storm, almost bare-masted, with only a small goose wing sail on the foremast to aid steering. They would lose, in a few hours, all the ground so hard won in many days of non-stop toil. Whenever the wind eased, even a little, they turned again, doggedly, striving to go westwards.

One sad morning, the 24th of September, in those awful conditions, poor William Leslie died. He was 22 years old and came from Huip, Stronsay, Orkney. The exact cause of his death was not known but it was entered in the ship's log as 'supposed consumption and wasting decease'.

The captain and the first officer made their way to the forecastle to supervise the sewing of the body into a canvas shroud. They found a saddened crew eating a frugal breakfast, acutely aware of the close presence of their dead shipmate. Wrapped in chain, Leslie's body was laid in the 'hospital', the place he so hated in life.

After a decent interval of several watches, the ship's company assembled in the lee of the forecastle for the burial at sea. Neither the men at the wheel nor the lookouts could be spared from their duties. The first mate read from the prayer book in place of the master as Captain Royal, too, was absent from the burial because his wife was so ill that she could not be left alone.

Spray lashed across the ship blotting out the words on the pages of the prayer book. The shriek of the wind, the creaking of the timbers, the shot-like whip cracks of the sails and the terrified screams of Denis the pig, served to remind one and all that they had even more important work to attend to. And so it was, with scant ceremony, that William Leslie's mortal remains slid into the cold, grey, angry waters of the Southern Ocean.

The crew returned to the grim fight for survival and the one thought common to everyone was the need to find a fair wind. When, at last, the wind moderated and shifted into the south, the *Springbank* and her crew had been fighting the roaring forties for six, whole, desperate weeks. Watches below, hot food and rest, were again possible, along with dry clothes. Just as life became easier and optimism returned, tragedy struck again.

Hannah Royal died on the 7th of October. She was 27 years old and she came from Liverpool. Again it was not known what her fatal illness was, but it was entered in the log as 'supposed consumption'. All through she had suffered from seasickness whenever the weather was bad.

Captain Royal was inconsolable. He kept saying that she was the best little pal he had ever had. In the last days of her life she knew that she was not going to recover. She had never liked the sea and she asked her husband to promise to bury her in the earth, not at sea. He ordered the carpenter to make a coffin as airtight as possible. When Mrs Royal's body was laid into it they filled it with flour and sealed it with canvas and pitch.

Sailing with death cast a gloom over the ship. Hannah Royal had been a very well-liked member of the ship's company. She was always friendly and helpful. Nonetheless, progress up the west coast of South America was good. With a fair wind on the port side the Juan Fernandez Islands were sighted on the starboard beam.

Those islands strike a special chord in the hearts of sailors. It was here that Alexander Selkirk was famously marooned, inspiring Daniel Defoe's classic tale of Robinson Crusoe. As the weather gradually changed from cold, to warm, to hot, little was seen of Captain Royal. He spent most of his time in his cabin, alone in his grief and leaving the running of the ship to his officers.

In the fierce heat of the tropics, west of the Galapagos Islands, they were becalmed in the doldrums. This gave them a new set of problems. The sun beat down mercilessly day after day. Supplies began to run low and the water ration had to be cut from one gallon per man per day to three quarts.

In contrast to the hurricane force winds of Cape Horn, they now set every stitch of canvas they could find to try and take advantage of every cat's-paw of wind. When the days of calmness ran into weeks the water ration had to be cut again, to half a gallon per day. To make matters even worse fever broke out.

The first victims were put in the 'hospital' in an effort to isolate the illness. Despite this the fever spread until half the crew were unable to turn out. With the heat and the stillness the *Springbank's* bottom became so fouled that when a light wind came she would not move. With a stronger wind, slowly, painfully, they got underway again and at long last they reached Cape St Lucas at the entrance to the Gulf of California.

Their destination, Santa Rosalia, was only 300 miles away. A southerly breeze would have them there in two or three days. But, not for the first time on this ill-fated voyage, the wind was dead against them. Captain Royal called a meeting of his officers because he was well aware that it might still take a long time to reach port.

The captain had a troubled mind. He was very mindful of his promise to bury his wife ashore and he was loath to break it. However, many weeks had passed since her death and interment of some sort was imperative. They already had fever on board and the stench of death, present in all parts of the ship, gave a grim warning of a further health hazard.

The officers, as always, supported their captain. They assured him that he had done everything possible to grant his wife's dying wish. They eventually persuaded him that they could no longer keep her remains on board. He, very reluctantly, agreed that she simply had to be buried at sea. And so it was.

It was as if a great weight had been lifted from Royal's shoulders but he had many problems to confront. More than half the crew was down with fever and the steward, no longer a young man, was ill too. The wind was in the north and they had to try, as best they could, to beat their way up the Gulf of California.

# Life on the *Springbank*

~ ~ ~

Everyone knew from experience gained in the North Sea and the Southern Ocean that, close hauled, the *Springbank* made as much leeway as endway. With her bottom fouled she was worse than ever. The Gulf of California is roughly 70 miles wide. With a brisk wind they could cross it in two watches, eight hours. In lighter winds it took several days. Either way it made no difference because they gained nothing whatsoever; they came back to the same landmarks again and again.

On the whole the crew preferred the lighter winds because it meant that they did not have to put about so often. A serious difficulty was that the *Springbank* would not go about. Her bow would come up to the wind but would not cross the wind. She would either fall off and stay on the same tack or, worse, she would stop dead and go into irons.

The only way to get the wind on the other side was to wear ship. That is, they had to turn away from the wind through 240 degrees. This put them on the other tack but in the process they could lose as much as four or five miles. In normal times all hands would be called to change tack, but now they sometimes had as few as seven fit men. The resetting of twenty or more sails under those conditions required a Herculean effort.

Despite the great need of the sick men, the water ration had to be cut again and no water was allowed for cooking. The sick men groaned and whimpered, tormented by thirst as well as their fever. The men still fit to turn out sucked and chewed on the buttons of their oilskins in an effort to stimulate a flow of saliva.

The temptation to put into the nearest port was great but never seriously considered for a number of reasons. It would be a breach of owner's orders. Owners took a dim view of their ships docking anywhere other than their preferred destination. With unreliable winds and their lack of manoeuvrability a safe berthing, without tugs, could not be guaranteed. Furthermore, with fever on board, they would face quarantine at any port of call.

Even at sea, Christmas was always celebrated. The cook would make a Christmas dinner with soft tack and a plum duff, and there would be an extra noggin of gin. However, that year on the

*Springbank*, Christmas passed without so much as a mention and without so much as a shanty sung while turning the capstan.

The agony continued and John Lund, the steward, got worse and worse until, on the 27th of December, he died. He was 58 years old and originally from Elsinore in Denmark but he lived in Leith. He apparently died of dropsy and heart failure. Like William Leslie and Hannah Royal he was buried at sea.

The new year of 1909 arrived unnoticed and it was not long until the day came when the pump had no more water to lift. What little water was left was taken out of the tank with buckets, cans and mops. Morale was at rock bottom and hope all but abandoned when, suddenly, the wind shifted.

Not only that, but it was a stiff breeze from the south, and almost before they knew it they were at Santa Rosalia. With a bold piece of seamanship Captain Royal took the *Springbank* straight in alongside. In double quick time food and water was taken on board and the officers and crew had their first cooked meal in over forty days.

The agent in the port could tell them that the Bank Line had given them up for lost and their next of kin had been informed. It was not surprising. They had made a total of 112 tacks in the Gulf of California and they had been at sea for 243 days.

Weeks later, and many thousands of miles away in Cullivoe, north Yell, Shetland, a meeting of the Women's Guild heard the news that the *Springbank* had arrived in Santa Rosalia. It was with a light step that the women hurried home to tell their families the good news.

*Author's acknowledgements:*

*The* Springbank *was sold to Norway in 1913 where she had a succession of owners. Renamed the* Arsyum *she had the distinction of being the first sailing ship to pass through the Panama Canal. She was scrapped at Stavanger in 1920. She had taken too much punishment from the sea to be repairable.*

*    In piecing the story of the voyage of 1908-1909 together I have had help from a great many*

*people and sources. I would like to say a sincere thank you to all of them. First of all, my father, the late Tom Tulloch, passed on what Uncle Nicky told him. Robert Anderson of Andersville, Cullivoe, over a quiet New Year dram, pointed me in the right direction to find more information.*

*Captain Andrew Anderson, also of Andersville, kindly read my efforts and gave good advice. His wife Netta gave me a photo of Uncle Nicky. Donald Silk of the Shetland Library took the trouble to find me a copy of the book* Crackerhash *and I am grateful to Joseph Stenhouse, the author of that fine book.*

*Radio Shetland gave me airtime and many people responded to my appeal for information. Cousins Tammy and Wilbert Irvine of Westsandwick gave me valuable information and encouragement and a photo of their relation who was on the* Springbank.

*The magazine* Sea Breezes *printed the letter that I sent to them and a number of readers contacted me, especially Mr Ernest Ashworth of London, who went to a great deal of trouble on my behalf. Mr Neil Staples of the Register of Shipping and Seamen in Cardiff did research for me.*

*Adam Robson gave me great encouragement. It is good to have the support of such a respected author. George Henry of Levie Cottage, Cullivoe, knew Nicky Tulloch; and the late Ian Anderson of Funafuti, Tuvalu was another nephew of Nick's.*

*Joseph Kay of Whalsay has shared his researches with me and has added greatly to my store of knowledge. Last but not least, Mr Harold Tait of Kirriemuir, a son of 'Springbank Lowrie', has made a huge contribution and has been able to correct some misinformation that I had.*

# 30

## Walkabout

THE NIGHT that poor Denis Cronin came together with Aquitino was a sad night that will be remembered forever in the quiet little town called Ballymor. Despite his Portuguese name, Pablo Aquitino was Irish, and a native of Ballymor. His ancestors had lived and worked there for more than a hundred years.

Manuel Aquitino had come to south-west Ireland in the 19th century. At that time there was no tradition of salting, drying and curing fish in this part of Ireland. As a Catholic nation the Irish were required, according to the teaching of the church, to eat fish on Fridays.

Plenty of fish were caught in the summer months but they were eaten fresh. However, in the winter and during spells of bad weather, fish was scarce and sometimes unobtainable. The good folk of Ballymor had to go without fish, but they could always make their peace with the priest because he would be without fish too.

At that time the most prominent citizen in the area was Major John Naysmithe-Hyde. Naysmithe-Hyde was a very rich Englishman who owned huge estates in Ireland as well as properties and vineyards in Portugal. He was also something of a philanthropist, prepared to improve the quality of life of the poor people who lived on his land.

The good major knew that Portuguese fisherman went far out into the Atlantic Ocean, some as far away as the Grand Banks of

116

Newfoundland, to fish for cod. Their catches were salted and dried. Not only did the fishermen have fish to last them and their families all winter, but they could sell fish to people who lived inland and even export fish to the neighbouring country, Spain.

It was in the 1870s that Naysmithe-Hyde took Manuel Aquitino to Ballymor and employed him to teach Irish fishermen the way to cure fish. Manuel never returned to his native Portugal. He fell in love with an Irish girl, married her, and the Aquitinos have been in Ballymor ever since.

Pablo Aquitino was born in 1961. He grew into a giant of a man, well over six feet tall, muscular, fit and as strong as an ox. He has a shock of blue-black hair and a full beard that grows high on his cheekbones No face or ears can ever be seen, only the coal black expressive eyes.

Pablo regards Irish, the Gaelic, as his first language, and he can sing the sad seonas (ballads) with feeling and emotion unbelievable in someone so big and rough looking. He is a fine dancer too and an all round musician but he is, above all, an accordion player.

He plays a press and draw, two-row, button accordion or, more often, a melodeon with just ten buttons in the one row. Pablo Aquitino is, by common consent, as good a player as anyone in Ireland and at the Fleadh Ceol in 1970 he won the All-Ireland Championship in the Junior Class.

As a teenager he was wild and reckless but highly intelligent. His father sent him to Dublin where he graduated as a teacher. It was the wrong career choice for him, he could never adapt to the restrictions and discipline of the classroom. After a number of 'final' warnings from his employers he quit teaching and for a time drifted aimlessly.

For a time he tried to make a living as a professional musician. He had some notable successes around the pubs and clubs in Dublin and across in England but he was wise enough to know that for him to continue this lifestyle was tantamount to committing suicide. Late nights and heavy drinking are very much part of this scene and he was never disciplined enough to resist either.

After returning to Ballymor he became a fisherman. Fishing is in the blood of the Aquitinos and for a time Pablo knew peace and contentment doing a job that he loved. At weekends he would take his accordion and go to the pub. Sometimes he would drink too much but it was not too much of a problem, he would sober up in time to go back to work on Monday morning.

Eventually he became bored. Much as he loved fishing he needed more adventure, more excitement and, abruptly, he went away; left Ballymor without telling anyone where he had gone. In fact he went to Portugal, where he still had relations, but what he did there was something that no one in Ballymor knew. What was obvious, when he eventually returned, was that he had made money, a lot of money.

He brought back a beautiful boat, the *Rosa*. It was sleek and fast, nine metres long and worth a small fortune. Rumour was rife, and the speculation was plentiful regarding the scource of Pablo's wealth, but he was very tight lipped on the subject. Politically he is a fierce Republican. He wants Ireland to be re-united and he strongly supports the Provisional I.R.A.

It did seem likely, however, that he had made his money gun running. His Portuguese friends and relations had contacts in the former Portuguese colony of Angola. A civil war had raged there for years and the whole country was awash with weapons of war. Given money, deadly weapons changed hands as freely as chewing gum. Using the *Rosa*, so the story went, Aquitino supplied the I.R.A. with tons of AK47s, mortars and grenades, and made a fortune so doing.

It was just the kind of dangerous enterprise that would give him the excitement he craved but, whatever the truth of the matter, Pablo was back, and declared his intention of staying for good. To underline this he, to the surprise of many, married Moya, the daughter of the much respected pub owner, Tim O'Sullivan. Many thought that Tim O'Sullivan had lost his senses when he allowed Aquitino anywhere near his beautiful daughter.

After a short time Tim retired and gave the pub over to Moya and Pablo. No money changed hands because Tim said that it was his daughter's inheritance and it pleased him to pass it on before he died. Those who thought the worst of Pablo expected him to be his own best customer in the pub, a disaster in the making.

All this did not alter the fact that Pablo had plenty of money. To show gratitude to his father-in-law he built him and his wife a beautiful new bungalow to enjoy their retirement in. He then put all his energy into the running of the pub and he built on to it a restaurant. Moya had been to catering college and she was a very able chef.

They gave the place a new name. Pablo still loved fishing and he wanted their pub to have a fishy name. On one of his musical adventures he had been to Teelin in County Donegal and had played in a pub called 'The Rusty Mackerel', so the name 'The Corroded Codling' was conjured up.

The Aquatinos and their business went from strength to strength. Every day Pablo went off in the *Rosa* and came back with a rich harvest of seafood to serve in the restaurant; beautiful lobsters, prawns, crabs, sea bass, wild salmon and lemon sole as well as other quality fish. 'The Corroded Codling' gained a reputation for quality that ensured a jam-packed dining room every night of the week.

So successful was 'The Corroded Codling' that it became the envy of every other business in the area. It was not only the food that made the place a success, Pablo was quick to exploit the famed Irish craic. Visitors to Ireland wanted, and expected, to hear traditional music in the pubs but it was very much a hit or a miss situation. Musicians gathered by chance and every session was entirely ad hoc.

Pablo changed all that by orchestrating the sessions. He asked musicians to come to the pub to play, especially on Saturday and Sunday nights. In return he paid them a small fee and gave them free drink. He got his money back because the guarantee of quality music attracted extra punters, both locals and tourists. The Aquatinos were superbly suited to what they did; they had to work hard but the rewards were considerable.

Pablo occasionally played in the sessions but quite often he would help out behind the bar and he was good at that too. He had great rapport with the regulars and if his quick wit did not deflate any awkward situation that developed then his sheer physical size did. Whenever he spoke the punters listened. He shamelessly used old jokes and clichés from the TV as if they were his very own inventions.

# The Foy and other folk tales

~ ~ ~

Old Seamus Brennen was one who always complained. It was in his nature to complain about the weather, the beer, the food or anything else that came his way. One night in the bar he was aware that he had got the first pint of Guinness from a new barrel. He declared that it was undrinkable and handed it back, but not before he had consumed about three-quarters of it.

"Sure, Seamus," said Pablo, "I'll give ye another pint o' porter."

Another pint was poured, allowed to settle, and topped up.

"Whit d'ye tink o' dis one, Seamus," asked Pablo.

Seamus took a sip from it and then held it up between him and the light. "It's a bit cloudy," he said, at last.

"Cloudy!" roared Pablo, "whit the hell d'ye expect for two pound, a bloody tunderstorm?"

Everyone, with the exception of Seamus, had fits of laughter. It was all part of the Aquitino magic.

In the fullness of time Pablo and Moya had three lovely children. The oldest, a boy, was called Tim after his grandad, and the two girls were called Mary and Anne. They were a happy and successful family except for one regular feature that Moya and the children dreaded: Pablo would go on a drinking binge.

It was not that he became nasty or ill tempered when he was drunk. He did not shout or swear, but he was totally irresponsible. He did no work but he went, as he said himself, walkabout, but always with his accordion. They might not see him for a week or more.

He would seek out old musical friends. They would play and sing for days on end. Sometimes much of the action would take place in 'The Corroded Codling'; sometimes they would go from pub to pub; sometimes they would go to other towns. At times like this Pablo Aquitino was totally unpredictable, eating and sleeping was very low on his list of priorities, drink and music was at the top.

The campaign, as he called it, would end when he came home filthy, exhausted and ill. He would mope around for a couple of days to recover before tackling work again with renewed vigour. Moya and the children hated the walkabouts. Mercifully they came seldom but, nonetheless, they dreaded the next time.

# Walkabout

~ ~ ~

On the fatal night, Moya knew that a walkabout was imminent the moment that Denis Cronin walked through the door. Denis was the man, above all others that Pablo liked and admired. He was Ballymor's most famous citizen. Thousands who lived far away from Ireland's shores knew him.

Cronin was a whistle and flute player, a singer and a song-writer. Success had come to him late in life. He had been invited to take part in a traditional music programme on TV and was an immediate hit. At the age of seventy-one he had embarked on a showbiz career that took him to all parts of Ireland as well as England, Scotland, the USA and Canada. For some unknown reason he attained pop star status in Germany.

Denis was home in Ballymor for a holiday and he had come to 'The Corroded Codling' for a Saturday night's music with his old friend Pablo Aquitino. Denis settled himself down among the other musicians and laid out his amazing array of whistles – one for each key – and his flute.

Another man in the pub that night was Patsy Callaghan. Patsy was a legendary local fiddle player and teacher, but while Denis had gone up in the world, Patsy had gone down. Patsy lived alone, he had no one to look after him, he seldom ate properly and his health suffered accordingly.

Patsy was a clever man who might have gone far but he chose a life of wandering through the countryside going from pupil to pupil giving fiddle lessons. He was a great teacher and he devised his own method of writing music but any money that he earned was spent in the pubs. Many a night he was so drunk that he had to be helped home.

Nonetheless, Patsy and Denis were delighted to meet up again. They were the same sort of age and they had made music together for more than sixty years. After talking to Denis for a time Patsy was the focus of a drama, he fainted and fell off a barstool. Many willing hands lifted him up again and put him back on his perch while others bought him glasses of whiskey, brandy and stout; enough booze to last him all night.

When he opened his eyes again and saw all the drink he thought, for a moment, that he had died and was in heaven. Until, that is, he saw Con Ryan sidling up to the bar. Con was another man who drank more than was good for him and he thought that maybe he could share Patsy's bonanza. He was well able to swallow anything that Patsy was unable to put away.

Patsy had lost none of his caustic humour. He fixed Con with a baleful, if somewhat bloodshot, glare and said, "Will ye bugger off and get yer own weakness!"

Pablo fetched his accordion and sat down beside Denis. "Bring me a double Powers and a pint of Murphy's," he shouted to the barman, "and whatever the boys are drinking."

Moya knew then, if there had been any doubt, that the walkabout was here with a vengeance. When the news spread that Denis, Pablo and Patsy were in a session in the pub the place was packed in no time. The only unhappy person was Moya. Already she was trying to plan how she would cope while Pablo was out of commission. But, she kept telling herself, she had seen it all before.

For hours on end there was a seemingly endless stream of reels, jigs and hornpipes but whenever the mood got quiet and reflective, Denis and Pablo would sing a song in the Irish language, a song that could bring a tear to the eyes of the sentimental listeners.

After the hour at which the pub should have closed Pablo got up and closed the outside doors. This was the classic shut-in, those who were inside could stay and anyone outside, including the Guards, was denied entry. The hour was very late and Denis declared that he was tired and sleepy and he was going home. Pablo tried very hard to keep him playing but in the end he was forced to accept that Denis was going home to bed.

"Oi'll drive you home, Denis," he said.

"Ye will not, Oi'll walk," answered Denis.

Pablo tried another tactic. "Oi'm going to check the ropes on the *Rosa* an yer house is on the way."

"Oi'll walk," said Denis, and strode towards the door.

Pablo would not take no for an answer. He grabbed Denis by the arm. "Why the hell will ye not go with me in the car?" he demanded.

"Oi tink ye shouldn't be drivin'. Oi tink ye've had too much to drink." He added, with a laugh, "After me livin all dis toime, Oi wouldn't want ta be killed by an eejut lik ye, so Oi'll walk."

## Walkabout

~ ~ ~

Denis left 'The Corroded Codling' and began his walk along the road towards his cottage. Aquitino went outside too and Moya followed, fearful of what might happen. She heard the squeal of tyres and was just in time to see Pablo drive past the front of the pub at high speed and disappear around the blind corner.

No sooner was he out of sight than she heard a dreadful crash and she knew that Pablo had run into the sea wall. Moya ran as fast as she could to the scene of the accident. When she got there her husband was down on his knees, he was weeping and making the most pitiful sounds of grief and anguish.

Moya saw that Pablo was cradling Denis Cronin's smashed and bloodied head in his arms and he was wailing, "Denis, Denis, if only ye'd come in the car with me ye'd be safe, Oi wouldn't have killed ye."

*This is a story of my own. It is based on some thinly disguised characters who live, or have lived, in Ireland.*

# 31

## The Minister and the Cow

THERE was once an old woman who lived alone, near to the hill land where the pasture was very poor. She could keep only one cow but that cow was the apple of her eye and she treated it like a child.

She was heartbroken when her beloved cow suddenly became very ill. The cow would not eat or drink or make any attempt to rise up to her feet. The old woman tried all the traditional cures but nothing did any good.

The cow got weaker by the day and it seemed that it was only a matter of time before she would die. One day the minister came to visit, he was new to the parish and the old lady had not met him before.

In many a village in those days the minister was the only person who had education, and a minister was expected to know a lot more than just Biblical matters. As soon as he arrived at the house the old woman demanded that he come to the byre and look at her poor sick cow.

The minister protested that he knew nothing of veterinary skills, he had come from a city and had seen few animals at close quarters. The woman would have none of it.

# The Minister and the Cow

~ ~ ~

She took him by the arm and pushed him firmly into the byre and right up to the dying cow.

He had no idea what to do but he picked a long straw from the floor and as he drew it up and down the cow's back he said, "If she lives she lives, and if she dies she dies, it but the brute beast anyway!"

With that he left the old woman to continue her vigil over the ailing cow. Almost immediately the cow showed signs of improvement. When the woman offered the cow a drink of warm water she mooed and drank some of it.

As the days went on the cow improved and before long she was outside grazing and fully restored to her customary good health. Her owner was overjoyed at the marvellous recovery.

A week later the old woman was at the village shop to buy her household needs. There she met a young girl who worked at the manse; a servant to the minister and his wife. When the old woman enquired after the health of the minister the servant had a sad story to tell.

The minister was very ill indeed. He had a boil in his throat, he had great difficulty in breathing and his life was in serious danger. He could neither eat nor drink or sleep and his wife was at her wit's end, she knew not how to treat him.

The old woman was deeply saddened that the man who had so miraculously cured her cow should have his own life in danger. She went home, dressed herself in her Sunday best clothes and made her way to the manse to see the minister.

She was met at the door by a servant who told her that the minister was far too ill to see anyone, but she refused to take no for an answer. She forced her way in and demanded to see the minister's wife. The good lady told her the same story but the woman insisted that she had to see the sick man.

At last she was shown upstairs and into the bedroom. The minister was lying in bed looking pale and ill. He was unable to speak but he nodded and tried to smile. The old woman went to the bedside and took, from under her shawl, a long, thick straw.

It was the very same straw that the minister had drawn over the sick cow's back. The woman did the same thing with the straw as she had seen the minister do.

"If he lives he lives, and if he dies he dies, it but the brute beast anyway," she intoned.

Although the minister was desperately ill he saw the funny side of the situation and it made him laugh. The laughter caused the boil to burst and the minister was able to breath easily again. And so began his recovery. He was soon restored to full fitness and the old woman was left convinced of the healing powers of the straw.

*This is another of my father's stories. I believed it to be a story from north Yell but my friend, Professor Bo Amqvist, tells me that he has heard it in Norway, Sweden, Finland, Russia, Denmark, Germany and Spain! There is also a poem that tells the same story.*

# 32

## St Patrick

AS ST PATRICK eased his BMW into third gear he looked in his rear view mirror and asked, "Are you alright in the back there, boys?"

So goes the modern joke about how St Patrick drove the snakes out of Ireland.

However, the man known to the world as St Patrick, the patron saint of Ireland, was, with typically Irish quirkiness, a Welshman.

From the time that he was a child, Patrick had a remarkable ability to control birds and animals. No animal ever attacked him and birds and animals were never frightened of him. He loved the wild creatures and he spent a lot of his time in their company.

Patrick was a dreamer and he was somewhat workshy. He had little appetite for the mundane, humdrum jobs that his father gave him to do. Any time he was given the opportunity he would walk along the shore and call to his friends – the seals and the otters.

They came to him by the dozen and he loved to lie in the warm sunshine with the animals rolling and playing in the sand near his feet. They trusted him entirely and seemed to know that he would never harm them. Patrick knew that whenever he arrived home he would get a row from his father because he had dodged the work.

In the summer of 401AD, when Patrick was sixteen, he fell asleep on a beach among his beloved seals and otters. He had taken a notion to explore and he had walked far away from home. Seals and otters had followed him and he had seen many deer and squirrels. He sat down on the beach to have a rest before he started the long walk home. The weather was hot and Patrick fell sound asleep.

He had no idea of how long he slept but he got a sudden and rude awakening. He heard the alarmed barks and splashes of the startled seals and when he looked up it was into the bearded and fierce-eyed face of a strange man. He had bare feet, a bare chest and he held a heavy wooden club in a most threatening manner above Patrick's head.

The stranger snarled what was clearly a threat. Patrick did not understand what he said but it was crystal clear that to try and make a run for it was not a good idea. When Patrick gathered his senses he realised that this savage man was a pirate. He had been well warned about pirates, they terrorised the coastline and he bitterly regretted wandering away from the safety of his own area.

The pirate grabbed Patrick by the hair and hauled him to his feet. With rough prods from the club Patrick was forced to walk along the beach and as they rounded the headland the pirate ship came into view. It was long and sleek and nearly black in colour and along each side were double banks of oars. Patrick knew little about pirate ships but he was aware that slaves manned the oars.

When the pirate galley came as close to the shore as it could Patrick and the pirate, who still kept hold of his hair, waded off to it but Patrick, being a small lad, was out of his depth and in danger of going under. He was hauled on board and viewed with total contempt. It was clear that the pirates considered him to be of little value. Nonetheless, he was chained to a vacant oar and the galley got under way.

The next week was by far and away the worst of Patrick's short life. At home he had been scolded and even punched by his father for being lazy, but the cruelty and brutality of the regime on the pirate ship was way beyond anything that he could ever imagine. His fellow slaves were whipped mercilessly. A walkway in the middle of the ship ran fore and aft. On it were the slave drivers.

The slave drivers were sadistic brutes who took a delight in flogging the helpless, wretched slaves. During Patrick's first day at the oars one slave collapsed and no amount of whipping could make him move. The slave drivers simply released his chains and threw him overboard without making any effort to find whether he was alive or dead. Patrick was to see, in the days that followed, this chilling procedure repeated several times. Life among the slaves was very cheap.

Patrick came in for his share of beating. Try as he might he could not row effectively. The oar was heavy and Patrick had no skill in handling it. He was out of time with the others and, truth to tell, he was more of a hindrance than a help. He fully expected to be dumped over the side because he was useless, but strangely enough the pirate who had captured him came to his rescue.

Although not the captain of the ship he was clearly a man of influence. He saw something in Patrick's character that he valued so he would not allow the slave drivers to flog him to death. Instead, he was taken away from the oars and put to work preparing food in the ship's galley. The food given to the slaves was disgusting slops, it was stale, sometimes rotten, and it contained little nourishment. They were fed mostly sids and low quality grain mixed with water, twice a day.

Slaves were given little rest either. They were seldom out of sight of land and during the hours of darkness rowing would stop for a few hours with just enough rowers to keep the ship on station. In his new job Patrick fared little better. The work was still unrelenting and a new problem came to him, seasickness. The smell of the awful food and the motion of the ship left him all but helpless and so he was threshed, kicked and beaten again.

Patrick lost all sense of time. He had no idea how long they had been at sea but one morning they put in to a port and the captain went ashore. Patrick had no way of knowing it but they were in the north of Ireland. The captain was a regular visitor here and he traded with the local chieftain, the mighty O'Neill. O'Neill provided the pirates with food and clothing while the pirates paid with stolen money, slaves or whatever they had been able to plunder.

Over much haggling Patrick discovered that he was to be part of the bargain. Although he was going into the unknown he figured that nothing could be worse than the pirate ship so it was with relief that he left her and walked, with an escort of O'Neill's men, to his new home. O'Neill was a rich and powerful man who kept many slaves and Patrick was billeted with the rest of them.

Life for a slave on O'Neill's estates was far from a happy existence. The work was hard, the hours were long and punishments for wrong doers could be severe. However, it was much, much better than it was on the pirate ship. O'Neill and his henchmen had discovered that if slaves were adequately fed then they got more work out of them; also, that severe floggings were counterproductive.

If a man was brutally flogged it could kill him or, at best, make him unfit for work for days on end. They also knew that if slaves were given work they were good at and enjoyed doing then they worked better. Indeed, they used the prospect of better jobs as an incentive and the fear of worse jobs as a deterrent. None of this was done for any humanitarian reason but it was known to be a more efficient way of managing slaves.

Patrick was put to work in the kitchens doing the most menial work. He was at the very bottom of the pecking order. He worked as best he could, his main aim to avoid the wrath of the head cook. Being of slight build and not physically strong he found the carrying of heavy cooking pots full of boiling water very difficult and several times he suffered quite bad burns.

Gathering and chopping wood for the hungry fires was another of his duties and every night, when he was finally finished work, he was completely exhausted and he slept deeply. Every morning he was aroused early and dragged from the pallet that he slept on. He wondered where the strength and energy was coming from to face another day of toil and drudgery. Any slowness was met with a kick or a punch.

For a time Patrick thought about how he could escape but other slaves strongly advised against any bid for freedom. Other land owners were always on the look out for runaway slaves and anyone caught on the run was indeed flogged to death as a deterrent to others. Patrick was deeply unhappy and spent any time he had to himself weeping and sobbing. However, one day an incident occurred that changed his life.

# St Patrick

~ ~ ~

Patrick was out gathering wood for the fire when one of the farm bulls ran amok. The bull had a crude ring in its nose that had got caught in a bush. With a gush of blood the ring pulled out and with a roar of pain the bull went mad. It gored and fatally injured one of the farm workers who looked after the animals. It charged, head down, and scattered the pile of wood that Patrick had built.

All the other workers ran for their lives but Patrick stood still and showed no fear whatsoever. He talked soothingly to the bull and soon it calmed down. Patrick went to the bull, stroked its neck and as quiet as a lamb it allowed Patrick to lead it by the ear into a pen. Not only that, but Patrick examined the bull's injured nose and suggested that it should be stitched together again.

O'Neill himself had witnessed this incident and declared that it was nothing short of a miracle. He immediately took Patrick from the kitchen and told him that from now on he would be working among the cattle, sheep and goats that were kept as farm animals. Patrick soon demonstrated that he could walk up to any animal and the animal had no fear of him; he could also herd them at will.

The winter that year was very severe. Blizzards were followed by hard frost and the snow was several feet deep. The farm animals fared very badly. They could be given some shelter but there was nothing for them to eat. Even the wild deer had difficulty in surviving. Those who did fed deep in the forest where the canopy had caught much of the snow, leaving the ground bare.

When the thaw finally came, O'Neill found that his herds had been decimated. He had lost more than half his stock and what was left was in a pitiful state. In the summer that followed the farm had a surplus of grass because so few animals were left to graze it and this gave Patrick an idea. He asked that certain meadows should be left to grow and not grazed at all.

At first O'Neill thought this a stupid plan but he had great respect for Patrick's talents so he allowed him to do what he wanted. Patrick believed that if the grass was harvested and dried it might be winter food for the cattle. Of course, they had no way of cutting the grass so it had to be plucked by hand and many slaves worked at this under Patrick's supervision.

Although the slaves had no say in the matter it was a job hated by them. The grass was home for thousands of snakes and workers were bitten hundreds of times. Patrick, because of his powers over creatures, was never bitten and he spent much of his time tending to the snakebites of others. After a few days the situation got so bad that O'Neill was ready to call a halt to the project, so Patrick had to think again.

As well as being able to attract wild creatures he could also repel them, so every morning he would go and clear the meadow of snakes. They all fled before Patrick's approach and snakebites were no longer an issue. As well as his power over animals Patrick discovered that he had instinctive knowledge of plants. By handling any plant, herb or fungi, he knew whether it was poisonous or if it had healing properties.

Therefore, in any isolated case of a snake bite, Patrick was able to apply a remedy to ease the wound. He also prepared concoctions to give to sick cows and had a lot of success. After two weeks of hard work they had plucked a large quantity of grass. Patrick ordered it to be spread out and turned over from time to time as it dried in the warm sun. When it had withered and was thoroughly dried it was stored away from the autumn storms and rain.

The following winter, while not as bad as the previous year, was severe too. Soon it was time to find out if the cattle would eat the dried grass and if it was nutritious. Patrick was delighted to find that the hungry cattle not only ate it, but also thrived. As long as the hay lasted they did not lose a single beast. For Patrick it was a triumph. In a short time he had changed from being the lowest of the low to being O'Neill's most valuable slave.

O'Neill gave Patrick many privileges and more freedom than any other slave had ever had. Nonetheless, he still saw himself as a slave and a prisoner, and he longed to get away and go home to his parents. One night he overheard O'Neill talking to his right-hand man. They were discussing Patrick and how valuable he was to them. Rather ominously, from Patrick's point of view, they agreed that he had to be closely guarded.

The news of Patrick's talents had spread. O'Neill reasoned that if Patrick was to escape and any of his neighbours caught him they would never hand him back, they would keep him and use him for their own benefit. Nonetheless, O'Neill was so impressed by Patrick's hay making experiment that he ordered his ironworkers to design and make long knives and mount them on wooden handles for grass cutting.

During the next few years O'Neill had enough hay cured to feed all his farm animals including the sheep and goats. He found that if by feeding them he lost none during the winter, he did not need so much stock. Patrick continued his work and O'Neill sometimes hired him out to neighbouring farmers to clear snakes off their land because they had all caught on to the benefits of hay making.

Patrick's life was to be profoundly changed by a visitor that came to see O'Neill. He had come from France; a monk by the name of Pierre, and he wanted to convert O'Neill and his household to the new religion called Christianity. O'Neill was bound by the unwritten rules of hospitality and therefore any visitor had to be given food and shelter. However, neither Pierre nor his teachings were to O'Neill's liking. O'Neill was a pagan and had every intention of staying that way.

O'Neill put Pierre into Patrick's care and he stayed in Patrick's quarters; no longer did Patrick live as a common slave, he had his own stone hut that he had made warm and comfortable. O'Neill would not allow Pierre to talk to any of his employees or slaves. Pierre quickly realised that he was wasting his time and that he was unwelcome, but he was tired from his travels and he needed rest. O'Neill grudgingly agreed that he could stay for a few days.

In Patrick's hut they had long conversations. Patrick had a burning desire to learn about Pierre's religion and, of course, Pierre was only too pleased to find a willing listener. Patrick asked millions of questions and among the things he learned was that Pierre knew Ireland well and had already converted some, in the south, to his faith.

On the penultimate night of Pierre's visit Patrick never slept at all, he lay awake the entire night wrestling with his thoughts. Pierre's message had made a lot of sense to Patrick and he was eager to learn more. For the first time in many months he saw a possible way of getting away from O'Neill and his life of slavery. When morning came he confessed his thoughts to Pierre.

# The Foy and other folk tales
~ ~ ~

Pierre was not at all willing to help him escape, for two reasons. Firstly, if they were caught it was certain, torturous death and, secondly, Pierre felt that he was breeching a bond of trust, as a guest, if he helped a slave to escape. However, he agreed that they had a really good chance of making a clean getaway because he had friends who would give them shelter in safe houses.

Patrick pledged himself, if he escaped, to become a monk and he promised to learn and preach and go to places far as a pilgrim. Pierre was most impressed by Patrick's earnest pleadings and at last he came to a decision. He would take Patrick away with him. He reasoned that the good that Patrick could do as a monk would far outweigh any ill that would be done to his conscience or to O'Neill.

The day that followed seemed to be never ending and there was no opportunity to plan or prepare for the bid for freedom. Patrick's mind was in turmoil and it was near impossible for him to do his usual work without showing his feelings. Somehow he got through the day without giving the game away and when night came there was little time to sleep.

Patrick and Pierre waited until everyone had settled down and for the darkest of the night before they set out. It was highly important that they put as much distance between themselves and O'Neill as possible and they had to have a secure place to hide during the next day. Pierre knew of no safe house that was close enough to help them. O'Neill kept bloodhounds so they waded for more than a mile through a river to put them off the scent.

For the last hour of the night they went westwards, at right angles to the way they wanted to go, in another attempt to avoid capture. At dawn they were deep in the forest and they chose a tree that was tall and had very thick foliage to hide in. There they stayed all day. Patrick slept a lot of the time. He was really tired, having had little sleep for the past two nights. They never knew whether O'Neill hunted them or not and they spent an entirely peaceful day.

Patrick found it hard to stay in the tree and be inactive. As a slave he had to work every day and he was unaccustomed to inactivity. They felt the pangs of hunger; they had not been able to take anything with them and the only food they found was a few wild berries. As soon as darkness fell they set out again with renewed hope, the weather was good and they made excellent progress. By morning they had reached the home of a friend.

Here they were given proper food and had the opportunity to sleep securely for the first time in several days. They did not travel the following night, they felt that they needed the rest. When they did move on they were well equipped and had with them enough food to take them to the next safe house. It was still far too risky to travel by day; O'Neill was a powerful chief and he had many spies all over Ireland.

At this point Patrick had the opportunity to look back on his time in Ireland. He had been a slave of O'Neill for six years. He was now twenty-two and fully mature and was full of optimism for the future. As they spent time together Pierre told him more and more of the Christian doctrine and Patrick had an insatiable appetite for the gospel. It was as if he had been waiting for this message all his life.

They were, of course, heading for the south coast of Ireland with a view to sailing to France where they would be beyond the reach of O'Neill or any of his supporters. In all it took them twenty days to reach the sea near Wexford but Pierre had friends there too so they were able to wait, in safety, for a ship with a captain who could be trusted to take them to the north of France.

Of O'Neill they heard nothing but, nonetheless, they were mighty relieved to reach the monastery in France that was home to Pierre. Patrick settled in and began his education as a monk and a preacher. His first problem was a serious one – he had to learn two new languages, French and the language of the Church, Latin. Patrick had no aptitude for languages and he struggled for years to master Latin.

It was, therefore, a very long time before he was able to preach because his Latin was so poor that no one understood what he was trying to say. Pierre had the utmost patience with him because he worked very hard at his studies. Other monks took an interest in Patrick's progress and as time went on, slowly but surely, he improved and the great day came when Pierre declared that, as a reward, Patrick would travel with him to England to preach there.

Patrick was delighted for several reasons. Life in the monastery was dull and the routine and discipline was very restrictive. More than anything Patrick missed being among the animals and birds. At the rare times he was allowed out of the monastery he was warned never to go into the forest because the animals there were so dangerous, especially the wild boars.

The monks never understood or saw the power that Patrick had over wild creatures and they kept him well away from what they saw as danger. Only once did Patrick get a trip to the shore to see the sea mammals that he loved so much. Patrick hoped for a number of things from his trip across the English Channel but above all he wanted to journey to Wales to see his parents again.

In England they spent many months walking from village to village preaching the Gospel and converting more and more people to the Christian faith. Pierre knew of Patrick's need to visit his parents. He accepted that what Patrick had in mind was, indeed, a visit. Patrick was entirely committed to his life as a monk. Therefore, they worked their way westwards and Patrick had a great thrill of anticipation when they crossed the border and stood on Welsh soil.

However, when they arrived at Patrick's home village it was a serious anticlimax because the house where he was born was now an empty ruin. Both his parents were dead and the rest of his family had gone away, no one knew where. For days Patrick mourned but he came to terms with the reality of the situation and, if anything, it made him more determined to be a success in the calling that he had chosen.

When the time came to go back to France it was like going home and Patrick knew, deep in his heart, he had no reason for going to Wales ever again. Over the years Patrick and Pierre journeyed together as missionaries to heathen lands. They had many adventures and faced, together, many dangers. But Patrick's life was to take another twist and it was because of an incident that happened near the monastery where they lived.

One day Patrick and the most senior bishop were out walking and discussing Patrick's next mission. They were walking along the edge of the woods in an area that was considered to be safe. Anton, who at fifteen was the youngest monk in the community, was gathering wild honey from a beehive in a hollow log. He disturbed the bees and they swarmed around his head causing Anton to run away.

In his panic he blundered into a nest of snakes – adders – and they were as angry as the bees. Out of the frying pan into the fire, Anton was in mortal danger. In a flash Patrick sized up the situation and ran to the rescue. With a wave of dismissal he confronted the snakes and they slithered off to escape Patrick's wrath. Next he commanded Anton to stand still, and he very gently removed each of the bees from the boy's skin.

The bees flew back to their hive. Not a single one had stung Patrick, and Patrick did not hurt a single insect. Anton had a few stings which Patrick treated and he was none the worse for his adventure. The bishop, however, was astounded. He looked on what Patrick had done as a miracle. He declared that anyone who could repel serpents – evil creatures, and attract bees – useful and industrious creatures, was a man apart.

He further declared that God favoured Patrick above all others and he immediately gave him the rank of bishop. Many hours of discussion followed. They had to decide how Patrick should spend the rest of his life. In the end it was left for Patrick to suggest the most valuable way forward and he decided that he would return to Ireland to convert his master of old to the new faith.

It was a high-risk strategy because it was known that O'Neill had resisted all overtures from the church; he was still a pagan. Patrick had run away and it could be that O'Neill still had vengeance in his heart. By this time Patrick had been in France for more than twenty years and he knew that O'Neill was now an old man. Patrick believed that to go back was a risk worth taking.

He knew if he succeeded such was the influence of O'Neill that many others would follow his lead. Besides, he believed that if he failed in his mission to Ireland then his entire ministry had been for nothing. His leader agreed that Patrick should follow along the path that God had shown him. He gave Patrick his blessing and sent Anton with him as a companion. Saying farewell to Pierre was hard, they had been through a lot together and there was no certainty that they would ever meet again.

# The Foy and other folk tales

~ ~ ~

It was a long and arduous journey from France to the north of Ireland and it seemed like a lifetime ago that Patrick and Pierre had made the journey in the opposite direction. Patrick had no idea what to expect when he reached O'Neill's stronghold. In fact, he had difficulty in finding anyone who remembered him, but the solemn and melancholy atmosphere of the household struck him as being remarkable.

The fact was that the mighty O'Neill, the greatest chieftain and warrior that Ireland had ever known, was lying helpless on his deathbed. At first Patrick was refused entry to the bedchamber but O'Neill was still conscious and he demanded to know who the visitor was. He remembered Patrick and he was amazed that anyone should be so bold as to return after escaping from slavery.

In the next few days Patrick sat at O'Neill's bedside and told the chief all that he had done since he left with Pierre. He talked earnestly of his unshakeable faith and how it could bring comfort to all who believed. When he was alone O'Neill reflected on his past life. It had been a life of power, violence, killing and stealing. Now, in his last days on earth, he began to regret some of the things he had done and he sent for Patrick to come back to his bedside.

He asked Patrick if repentance and forgiveness were possible for him given the fact that he had never forgiven anyone in his life. Patrick assured O'Neill that it was never too late to say sorry and taught the great man to pray.

Patrick spent many hours at the bedside of the dying chief. Indeed he was with him when he breathed his last, some six weeks after he arrived back. Patrick conducted the funeral service. O'Neill was given a Christian burial and many marvelled at the change brought about by the lowly ex-slave.

And so it was that Christianity came to the north of Ireland. O'Neill's son and heir embraced the faith and Patrick was given leave to roam the countryside and preach to O'Neill's people. A new attitude of tolerance and kindness prevailed around the O'Neill estates.

Patrick consolidated his position. He was well aware of how easy it was for converts to slip back into the old ways. He built his first church at Armagh; an important location in the Irish church to the present day. He trained priests and put Anton at the head of them while he travelled far and wide preaching to the people.

While Patrick was highly respected as a 'holyman' he was best remembered as the slave who could clear the snakes from the land. At first Patrick was annoyed by this, he felt that to spread the word of God was far more important but, in time, he realised how important it was to the poor farmers and peasants who made their scant living from the land, and he became more sympathetic to their demands.

For many years Patrick wandered the length and breadth of Ireland and everywhere he hounded the snakes until they became fewer and fewer. At last the time came when Patrick knew in his heart that all the snakes had gone. In no corner of Ireland was there a single snake left and Patrick felt that he had to make a supreme effort to make an announcement to the whole world.

He was no longer a young man but he embarked on the climb to the summit of the mountain now known as Crow Patrick. It was a holy place to the pagans and to the Christians and the perfect pulpit for Patrick to preach the sermon of his life and declare Ireland to be free from evil serpents. The climb, however, was desperately difficult for the ageing monk.

He insisted on climbing in his bare feet. The mountainside was rough with many sharp and loose stones that cut his feet to ribbons. With dogged determination he plodded onward and upward, often having to rest. His helpers offered to carry him but he refused all offers of help and by the time he reached the top his strength was gone, but he drew on his last reserves and delivered his sermon in a strong but wavering voice.

Not only did he declare that Ireland was free of snakes but he declared that all Ireland was a Christian island. He finally declared that his mission was complete. It was thirty years since he had returned to Ireland to convert O'Neill and he was now seventy-five years old. He said that any time that was left to him would be spent in rest and meditation and in preparing himself for the Hereafter.

Patrick returned to Antrim where he lived for another year. He died peacefully in the year 461 at the place now called Saulpatrick. He was buried near the church that he built in Armagh. His brother monk and great friend Anton conducted his funeral service.

*This story is largely my own invention. Little is known for sure about St Patrick so I took the liberty of writing it the way I think it might have been.*

# 33

## The Portuguese Fisherman

FOR AS far back as anyone knew the men folk of the Christianho family had been fishermen. Not only was it in their blood but also, in their part of north-west Portugal, there were few other ways to scrape together a living.

Over the years fishing methods had changed but two things remained the same: fishing was a hard, dangerous way of life, and fishermen earned little; they were poor people.

In the 18th century big factory ships took fishermen far out in the Atlantic Ocean, out as far as the Grand Banks of Newfoundland where cod was plentiful. Those ships carried numerous, small, open, one-man boats called dories, that were launched every day, weather permitting.

Individual fishermen rowed off in them with fishing lines and bait, returning at night with their catch to be salted down in barrels and eventually dried. Fishermen were paid according to what they caught and while they earned little, ship owners and fish merchants were often rich men.

Fog on the fishing grounds was a common occurrence. The Grand Banks is a place where warm air from the south meets the cold air drifting down from the Arctic. Fishermen had to be vigilant; at the first signs of poor visibility they hauled in the lines and made all speed back to the ship.

~ ~ ~

At home in Portugal each autumn, wives and families eagerly awaited the return of the ships. It was the highlight of the year. Everyone flocked to the harbour to meet his or her loved ones.

However, when the *Nina* returned, the captain came ashore himself and took Rosa Christianho back to her cottage. Without having to be told, everyone knew that something awful had happened. Rosa's husband, Manuel, was a fisherman on the *Nina*.

It was the sad duty of Captain Diaz to break the news that Manuel had been lost on the Grand Banks. Not only that, but the circumstances were particularly tragic. One afternoon, when all the dories were out fishing as usual, a dense fog came down and reduced visibility down to a few metres. The fishermen returned one by one and within the hour they were all safely back on board except Manuel. Captain Diaz ordered that the ship's siren be sounded every thirty seconds.

Next day the fog was as bad as ever. They continued to sound the siren but of Manuel there was no sign. The fog persisted for three whole days. As soon as it lifted the *Nina* began a systematic search, but Manuel and the dory he was in had disappeared without trace.

Eventually the hope of finding Manuel faded and finally died. Other fishermen were heartbroken. They could imagine all too vividly the horrible death that Manuel had faced. Barring a miracle he would die of cold and exposure, alone and without help of any sort.

Mrs Christianho accepted the dreadful news with the quiet resignation of one who had faced tragedy before. She could well remember the time when her older brother had been lost at sea. Captain Diaz was a kindly man and he fully understood the plight that Rosa Christianho and her four children faced.

However, he was very limited in what he could do to help her in the absence of any welfare services. Not only did he pay her in full for Manuel's share of the catch, but he also told a few white lies. He falsified the books to show that Manuel had caught more fish than was, in fact, the case.

By so doing he was able to pay the widow a little more money than she was entitled to. He also gave the family a quantity of salt fish to help them through the winter. His final offering was a promise that he could keep Manuel's berth on the *Nina* open to the oldest of her sons, fourteen-year-old Luis.

To see her son stepping into the shoes of his father was the very last thing that Rosa Christianho wanted but, with calm dignity, she thanked the captain. She knew, in her heart of hearts, that there was no alternative; to keep a roof over their heads and food on the table they had to have a breadwinner.

For his part Luis was ready to grow up. He had often day-dreamed of the time when he would go to sea as a man, but, of course, he never thought that it would be brought about by the loss of his father's life.

During his first season on the *Nina* Luis was not allowed in any of the dories. The captain kept him on board the mother ship where he washed, split and salted the fish. With dry bright weather fish was taken out of the salt and hung up on long lines to dry, but they had to be taken in quickly if it rained. This, too, was part of Luis's duties.

At the end of the season Luis was paid off with a modest amount of money. He had been a hard worker. Captain Diaz and the ship's officers had found him to be smart and respectful and he was offered a place for the following summer. But Luis was not satisfied with his job on the ship, he wanted to fish.

He asked Captain Diaz to give him a dory and his opportunity came when one of the fishermen became ill. Out on the ocean all by himself, Luis had time to think. He knew how little fishermen got paid and he knew how well off, by comparison, Captain Diaz, a part owner of the *Nina*, was.

Over time he developed a burning ambition to be more than just a fisherman. He was determined that one day he would be like Captain Diaz or even better off; one day, he vowed, he would have his own ship. He knew, however, that the only way to succeed was through hard work.

He fished like a man possessed. He was never on board the *Nina* except during the short summer nights. He fished continuously through weather fair and foul and at the end of the season he had more money than anyone else on the ship.

When he got home he confessed to his mother his ambition. He gave her all the money he had earned and she agreed to save as

much of it as possible. To earn more money he persuaded the captain to lend him a small boat to enable him to fish inshore during the winter. It was a mild winter and Luis lost no opportunity to be off fishing. His winter fishing proved to be amazingly successful and he was able to save some more money.

He was entirely single minded in his efforts to fulfil his ambition. He never went into the taverns and he didn't spend money unless it was necessary. He did have a girlfriend and she was another reason for his drive. He was determined that he would never ask his lovely Anna to marry him unless he could offer her comfort and prosperity.

After three years, his younger brother Pablo became a fishermen too. He soon got caught up in Luis's dream of bettering himself. Later, when the youngest of the Christianho boys, Jaime, joined them on the *Nina*, the whole family was obsessed with making money.

With the careful management of their mother they saved a sizeable amount. It was a proud day for Rosa when they were able to buy a one-fifth share in the *Nina*. Her late husband Manuel had been a good man, loving and caring, but he was born a fisherman and had no thought or ambition that he could ever be anything else.

The share in the *Nina* marked a huge change for Luis. He was no longer fishing from a dory; he was now a junior officer serving as an apprentice under the watchful eye of Captain Diaz. He learned the art of sailing, man management and navigation, and took to it like a duck to water.

With his drive and energy fishermen worked harder than they had ever done before and for three years on the trot they were the first ship home, with a full hold of fish. Consequently they got the best prices. From here there was no stopping Luis Christianho.

Some admired his ability and single mindedness, others saw him as plain greedy, but he went on and on. All the money he earned he invested in the *Nina* until, when Captain Diaz retired, Luis became the captain and he and his brothers owned the ship with no other shareholders.

After another few seasons Pablo and Jaime became bored by the grind of hard work, they wanted an easier life. But there was no let up with Luis; he worked as hard as ever. When his brothers complained, Luis bought them out too, but he had to borrow heavily from the bank and pledge the *Nina* as collateral.

And so, at the age of twenty-six, Luis Christianho was the captain and the sole owner of the *Nina*. He married his lovely Anna, they had very grand wedding and they moved into a big house; a house so beautiful that it was beyond the wildest dreams of any ordinary fishing family.

Next season Captain Christianho and the *Nina* went back, with renewed vigour, to the Grand Banks. With his drive and experience and good fortune they had a record season and they were back home with a full cargo of prime cod sooner than any ship had been before.

Even so, Luis still owed the bank a great deal of money for the purchase of the *Nina* and his new house. Some other ship owners approached him and asked if he was willing to accept a charter to take a cargo of salt out to the ships that were still fishing. Never one to turn down the opportunity to make money he quickly agreed.

It occurred to him that if he was going back to Newfoundland he might as well do some extra fishing. He was, therefore, keen to trans-ship the salt as quickly as possible. It was late in the summer and the weather was poor. There were winds approaching gale force and heavy seas.

In his hurry to do more fishing, Captain Christianho was guilty of a serious misjudgement. To discharge the salt he opened his hatches at sea, not taking the time to seek shelter, and almost immediately the *Nina* was swamped by a huge wave that broke across the ship.

The hold, the forecastle, and everywhere below decks filled with seawater and within minutes the *Nina* foundered. Because they were close to another ship – the intended recipient of the salt – there was no loss of life, but Luis Christianho had to return home in someone else's ship, as a passenger, a broken man.

Everything he had toiled for in twelve hard years had gone. Not only was he penniless but he also had a serious debt problem. He had to surrender the house and he and Anna had to live with Rosa. She was willing enough to have them but, to the whole family, the loss of the *Nina* was a devastating blow.

Fishing was all that Luis knew. He was forced into the humiliating experience of begging for a berth as a humble fisherman on another ship. He had to confront the reality that he was going to be deep in debt for the rest of his life. A friendly skipper took pity on him. Luis had gone full circle and was back almost where he started, fishing from a dory.

Gone, too, was his ambition and energy. He cared not whether he caught fish or not. He had to be forced from his hammock and pushed into the dory. The captain told him that if he were unwilling to try then he would not retain him for another season. Luis could not care less, he even considered suicide.

One day when he was supposed to be fishing he lapsed into a mood of apathy. He was thinking that his father was right, if you were born a poor man then that was how you should stay and be contented with your lot in life. He reproached himself for being conceited and bringing false expectations to his mother and wife.

When he emerged from his black swoon he saw that the fog had come. It was thick and dense and visibility was no more than thirty metres. Even then he did not care. He thought that this was what had happened to his father and while his father deserved better, he did not. He was resigned to die in the same manner as his father.

For two nights and a day the fog was unrelenting. However, when the daylight came in after the second night, the fog cleared and the clear sky allowed the sun to warm Luis's chilled body. As the last bank of fog dispersed Luis could see, in the distance, a ship, but it was unlike any ship he had ever seen before.

It was grey, gaunt and ghostly and it was wallowing drunkenly in the slight swell. It had no sails save a few rags of shredded canvas, and some rotten strands of frayed rope hung from masts unsupported by any stays or rigging. With a feeling of awe and dread Luis rowed his dory towards the stricken ship.

It was clear that the ship was derelict. It was waterlogged and floated deep in the water almost on its beam-ends. As Luis got nearer to it he kept looking over his shoulder and, over him, came the uneasy feeling that he had seen this ship before. Certain aspects of her looked familiar.

He was in a state of the highest excitement when, from a distance of fifty metres, he could read the washed-out nameplate on the stern. It said *Nina*. His ship. Luis could not believe his eyes, it was his ship re-floated, it was a miracle. So overcome was he that he sat at his oars, he didn't know for how long, trying to believe the unbelievable.

With trembling hands he tied the dory to the ship and cautiously climbed on board. Other than the fact that the sails and rigging were all gone the *Nina* seemed undamaged and it was clear that she could be repaired and restored. He sat down to try and understand what had happened.

Still in a brown study he heard voices shouting his name. It was the ship that he fished from, the *St Theresa*, come to investigate the hulk. Among them they solved the puzzle. When the *Nina* sank it was the salt that took her to the bottom. She was an all-wooden ship so that when the salt washed out of her the buoyancy of the timber took her back to the surface.

Captain Oliveira of the *St Theresa* gave Luis six men and enough sails and ropes to get her underway again. When she was pumped out the *Nina* floated on an even keel and began to look something like her old elegant self again. Luis became Captain Christianho again and he sailed her back in triumph to Portugal.

The *Nina* was re-fitted and freshly painted all ready for another season and the fortunes of Luis Christianho were restored. Now, however, it was a very different Luis who sailed to the Grand Banks of Newfoundland the following summer. Gone was the brashness and obsessive greed to make more and more money.

He had learned humility and, for the first time in his life, appreciated just how lucky he was. He became a kindly man who was ready to help anyone who was less well off than he and he was the most loved and respected citizen in the fishing community.

*It is so long since I heard this story that I cannot remember where it came from. Neither can I remember the names of the fishermen or the names of the ships. Therefore, I have taken author's licence to fill in names and detail.*

# 34

## The Denschman's Hadd

AFTER Shetland became part of Scotland in 1469, people were plagued and sorely harassed by raiders and pirates. When Shetland was a part of Norway and Denmark they were well protected, but Scotland had a hard enough task protecting themselves, let alone a place like Shetland that they put little value on.

Some of the pirates came from Scotland but the most ruthless and efficient raiders came from Viking stock. They had run out of new places to plunder so they turned on the folk of places like Shetland who were of the same race as themselves. One of the most feared raiders was a frequent visitor to the island of Unst.

He came from Denmark but no one knew his name or anything about him. He was known, simply, as the Denschman and every resident of the island was terrified when his ship was sighted. The very sight of his ship, the *Erne*, put dread into the hearts of all who saw her. *Erne* – the Norse word for eagle – was black and sleek and laden with menace.

Whenever the *Erne* was sighted the Unst folk watched to see where the Denschman was going to land because they had to make sure they kept well out of his way. The pirates were too many and they were too well armed to resist; they were also utterly ruthless and would strike down anyone who stood in their way. Unst folk took to the hills and the banks and allowed the pirates free rein.

The raiders would go from farm to farm and croft to croft taking anything of value that the udallers had. When the *Erne* was seen to leave, people would creep back to what was left of their homes and try, as best they could, to get on with their lives. They would curse the Denschman and the *Erne* but they knew, in their hearts, that it was only a matter of time before he came back to devastate their island yet again.

One midsummer brought severe and unseasonable weather; storm force winds from the north-west and mountainous seas. When, at last, the wind eased down to a gentle breeze, but the seas were still running high, the terrible news came that the *Erne* had been seen off the north of Yell behind the Holm of Gloup.

Men were sent to the high hills of Vallifield and Saxavord to keep a look out. Sure enough, the *Erne* was seen to approach the west coast of Unst between Hermaness and Widwick. The oldest udaller was among the watchers and he declared that the Denschman would have to go around Muckle Flugga, the northernmost point of the island. Any vessel trying to land on the west coast would, without doubt, be smashed to pieces on the rocks.

A respected seaman agreed with him but it was his opinion that the Denschman was far too wise and too skilled a seaman to make any mistake. As they watched, and as the *Erne* came closer, they saw that all was not well with the pirate ship. It was low in the water, it was sluggish and it did not obey the helm. Hope rose in the hearts of the Unst men. If the *Erne* was wrecked that might be the end of all their troubles.

The *Erne* was driven in towards a treacherous shore that was strewn with baas, crags and sharp rocks. For a time it looked as if the Denschman was attempting to beach his ship on the Ayre of Widwick. This was not, by any means, a safe landing but it offered the possibility of at least some of the men saving their lives. It was not to be. As the Unst men prayed for the destruction of the pirate ship, it was as if their prayers were immediately answered, because the wind veered.

The *Erne* struck the Holm of Widwick with a sickening crash that tore a gaping hole in her side. This was a fatal wound but she bounced back off the rocks and was carried in by the wind, the tide, and the sea, to her doom on the rocks of Flubersgerdie. The *Erne* began to break up and it seemed impossible that any man aboard could survive such a total shipwreck.

"Praise the Lord," cried the old udaller. "He has delivered us from the evil Denschman!"

The Unst men all went home to spread the good news and there was great rejoicing that they were finally rid of their evil tormentor. There was also the prospect of salvaging wood from the wreckage and perhaps other valuables as well. They eagerly waited for the high seas to calm down so they could revisit the scene of the wreck.

After two more days the sea was smooth and men launched a boat from the beach at the Westing. Sure enough, there was plenty of wood either washed up or floating near the shore. They spotted a long plank in a sea cave but when they went into the cave to take it they saw a terrible sight.

On a ledge high above the sea stood the Denschman. Somehow he had survived the wreck and it seemed likely that he had used the plank as a makeshift ladder to climb on to the ledge. He had his sword in his hand and he looked well and strong. He didn't speak but he was haughty, defiant and he gazed down at them with utter contempt. The Unst men were shocked but they knew he could not harm them.

The pirate was a prisoner in the cave. To dive into the sea was instant death because below were sharp jagged rocks; further into the cave the ledge petered out and above was an overhanging cliff that was impossible to scale. Nonetheless, they went home early to tell the news that the Denschman was still alive and every day for the next two weeks they went to the cave to see if he had fallen to his death.

Not only did he continue to survive but always looked the same. He seemed none the worse for the cold and the lack of food. They were certain that nothing eatable existed in that damp cold place. Because of all the harm he had done to them they felt no pity for the plight of the Denschman and were quite prepared to watch him die a slow miserable death.

However, many of the womenfolk did not agree. They knew how wicked and evil the Denschman was but they did have it in their hearts to forgive him. One of the women spoke on behalf of them all.

"What kind of men are you?" she asked. "How can you watch a human being die such a horrible death? You must put an end to this matter. Either rescue the pirate or kill him and put him out of his misery."

The men were uneasy and they held a meeting to decide what they were going to do. As usual the oldest udaller had the last word. He declared that they had to kill the Denschman. It was far too dangerous to set him free. He also said that they would take his boat because it was bigger and it would carry an extra couple of men.

The next morning the men armed themselves with pitchforks, sickles, tullies and a boatload of stones to throw at their target. They were utterly determined to put an end, once and for all, to their hated enemy. When they assembled at the beach they stopped in their tracks because the old udaller's boat had disappeared. It was unthinkable that anyone on the island would steal a boat so they began to fear the worst.

They launched another boat but they were not at all surprised to find the cave empty. The Denschman had disappeared. How he had managed to escape was a mystery but none doubted that he had made his getaway in the old udaller's boat. Such was his skill as a seaman he would certainly survive the long journey to safety in a small boat and live to tell the tale.

When the men returned home a great gloom and dread settled over the island. They all believed that the Denschman was certain to return and when he did he would take terrible vengeance for the way that he had been left to die in the cave.

Months passed without any word or news of the pirate and it was more than a year later that a strange ship appeared in Bluemull sound. It was a black vessel that bore a marked resemblance to the *Erne*. The Denschman had returned. As the ship came closer they could see that at the masthead a white flag – a flag of truce – was flying. Never in the past had the pirate made any attempt at disguising his intentions, a blood red banner was his usual colour. The white flag really did mean, amazingly, that he came in peace.

# The Denschman's Hadd

~ ~ ~

The ship dropped anchor in the Westing bay and four brave men rowed off to it from the beach. When they came near they saw that the boat tied to the stern of the ship was the one belonging to the old udaller. The Denschman himself stood on the deck and addressed them in a stern voice. He commanded them to untie the boat and give it back to its rightful owner.

"You will find that the boat is laden with goodly gifts for his three fair daughters," he said, "they will know why I give them those tokens. Begone and know that no more will I harm you."

So saying, he upped anchor and sailed away on the southerly breeze. The boat was unloaded and all the Denschman's gifts were laid out on the beach. There were utensils of gold and silver, ornaments, silk and linen, rich wine and fruit, as well as much precious grain. The old udaller gazed in wonder as did many others but the three daughters hung their heads in shame and blushed deeply.

"What is the meaning of this," demanded the udaller of his daughters.

The two younger girls fell on their knees and clasped their father's hand while the older one spoke in a low voice. "I will tell you father, but please forgive us and please do not be angry. It lay heavy on our hearts that a defenceless man with such a bold spirit should die in the cave like an otter caught in a snare. We went to the banks in the darkest hours of the nights and lowered a basket with food to keep him alive. We could not bear the thought of you killing him so we stole your boat and gave him a rope to lower himself down. He promised that he would never raid Unst again and we know that he will keep his word."

"I forgive you," said the old udaller. "What would come of us poor men if lasses were not pitiful?"

The Denschman did, indeed, keep his word and ever after that he brought benefit to Unst and never harm.

*I got this story from my friend Tom Muir of Orkney. A version of it was published in a journal in 1886 and Elizabeth Morewood of Mid Yeli tells yet another version.*

# 35

## The Laird of Gloup

HORACE Saxby, the Laird of Gloup, was among the last of the traditional lairds. He was, indeed, monarch of all he surveyed and had total control over his tenants. As he saw it, it was his right. If he needed work of any sort done he sent for some of the crofters and gave them their orders.

Saxby's estate was small and somewhat isolated and situated at the very north of the island of Yell. He lived with his long-suffering wife in the Haa of Gloup and they drove around Cullivoe on their BSA motorcycle that had a sidecar attached.

The laird, in his young days, had been something of a wild colonial boy. He had served as an officer in the Royal Canadian Mounted Police, the famous Mounties.

Once, when he and another Mountie, also a Shetlander, were out on patrol they were caught in a severe blizzard. So bad was it that they were seriously concerned as to their survival. It was a total whiteout, they could see nothing at all and they lost all sense of direction. To make matters even worse they quarrelled about which way they should go. When no agreement could be reached they split up and each went their separate way.

Saxby survived, just. His experience had been so bad that he resigned his badge immediately and left Canada for good. He left not knowing what happened to the friend he had left in the snowstorm, but he firmly believed that he had perished in the cruel winter weather.

It seemed that Saxby was determined never to allow the like to happen to him again, because the next we know of him was that he was a policeman in East Africa. Whatever the hazards and dangers to be faced in Africa, to die in a blizzard was highly unlikely to be one of them.

Fully forty years after his near shave in Canada, and when he had retired to Gloup, he went one day to the Greenside shop. Imagine his amazement when he saw, standing at the counter, his friend the Mountie who he had parted with all those years ago in the snow. Each had believed the other was lost and it was an extremely happy reunion. They both agreed that Yell was a far safer place than northern Canada.

Saxby was a true eccentric and many stories are told about him; stories that live on in the north Yell store of local history and anecdotes.

In those days three or four gates punctuated the road to Gloup. Mrs Saxby used to sit on the pillion of the motorbike rather than in the sidecar and it was her job to open and close the gates. One day, when Saxby arrived at the post office, he was horrified to discover that his better half was missing. What had happened, of course, was that in his hurry to get to the post office he had not given her time to get back on the bike. He turned in a panic and drove back towards Gloup like a madman.

On his way to the first gate he overtook one of his neighbours who was walking along the road. "Have you seen my wife?" he roared.

When he got no response he shouted all the louder and his anger and frustration was complete when the neighbour calmly swung his leg over the bike and sat down on the pillion. Saxby had, in his panic, forgotten that his neighbour was profoundly deaf, and thought he was being offered a lift!

During World War Two, Saxby was a lieutenant in the Home Guard. Once there was a rumour that the Germans had landed in West-A-Firth. This is the uninhabited area of Yell across the voe from where the Saxbys lived.

It was the middle of the night but all the men of the Home Guard were called out and Saxby was going to lead a patrol to find the invaders. However, it came to nothing for two reasons; there were no Germans in West-A-Firth, and Saxby had forgotten to put in his false teeth so no one could understand a word that he said!

The Laird of Gloup was well aware of his duty as a landowner and noblesse oblige so he took part in some of the local social life. He had some musical talent and one day he arrived at the house of Willie Barclay Henderson, one of his tenants, in a state of considerable agitation.

Doing nothing in particular a tune had come in to his head. He set out at once to see Willie, humming the tune all the time in case he lost it. Willie got out his fiddle and managed to learn the tune. It is still played a lot in north Yell and beyond. It goes under the name of 'Gloupie'.

The laird also wrote songs that were performed in local concerts. His best remembered song is called 'Slippery Pete'. It is about a black man with huge feet and while it is not racist in any nasty way it is so politically incorrect that nobody would dare to sing it nowadays.

It seems that Willie Barclay Henderson was Saxby's right hand man around Gloup. In the fullness of time Willie bought Gloup but, needless to say, he was a very different sort of a laird.

As laird, whenever Saxby needed something done, it was to Willie that he went first. One day he announced that he wanted a concrete gate post constructed. Four of the tenants gathered and built a shuttering to pour the concrete into. Cement was none too plentiful and Willie suggested to Saxby that it would be useful if they had some reinforcing to strengthen the post.

Saxby went home and returned with an armful of African spears, relics of his time in Kenya. The spears were stuck into the earth, in the hole dug for the post, and the concrete was run around them. It worked because the post is still there after all these years.

While the men were making the post Saxby entertained them with stories of his time in the colonies. He told them that once, when he was in East Africa, there were two men repairing a boat. They had with them a huge iron kettle that they intended to melt pitch in but the mosquitoes were so fierce that they had to take cover under the upturned kettle.

After a time the mosquitoes began to bore holes in the kettle and their sharp beaks appeared through the iron. The men each had a riveting hammer and every time a mosquito's nose appeared on the inside of the kettle they flattened it over and riveted it to the iron.

"This went on for quite a while, then," Saxby said, "by jingo, they flew away with the kettle!"

*The late Willie Barclay Henderson was my father-in-law. I heard these stories of Saxby from him one night over a dram.*

# 36

## The Cannonball

THE HAA of Midbrake in north Yell, where I was born and spent the first thirteen years of my life, was a great place for children to play on a rainy day. It was full of nooks and crannies, cupboards, blind windows and a garret with spacious eshins.

The garret was my favourite place. One half of it was a bedroom but no one slept there regularly, the other half was full of all kinds of junk. There was a big wooden tub full of glass floats, a gearbox that had done duty in a car, a semi-rotary pump, and a cabinet encrusted with precious looking stones, that advertised Fairy dye.

There were boxes and boxes of nuts, bolts and brackets, a rakki from a sixtreen, herring floats, barrel hoops, rope, an old coutched sail, baits kuddies, five or six wheels and spinnies as well as much miscellaneous trumpery. The skylights provided a lofty overview of the entire neighbourhood.

One place that I seldom ventured was under the stairs. It was accessed through a closet that opened off the kitchen and in it were rubber boots, coats, jackets, staffs, a peat box, the cat's dish and much more.

The entire bottom flooring of the house was flagstones and anyone who penetrated deep in to the closet through the solid curtain of outerwear was rewarded with the dank smell of the earth that rose up through the gaps between the flagstones.

# The Cannonball
~ ~ ~

There were two other things in the closet, and for years I believed them to be a single object, or at least that they belonged together. The base consisted of a heavy stone some ten inches square and six inches deep. The centre had been chiselled out to make it into a bowl.

Lying in the hollow of the bowl was a rusty iron ball that was slightly bigger than a cricket ball. To begin with I did not have the strength to lift the stone but one day I managed to drag it into the kitchen. But I got little thanks for my efforts and I was told to put it back again.

When I tried to do as I was told the ball rolled away from the stone and I asked my father what the stone was for.

"Yon's a grice truggel," he said. "Dey wir med heavy lik yon so dat da peerie grices couldna ding dem ower."

"What wis da baa fur?" I asked

My father had a gleam in his eye that told me he relished the question.

"Yon's da cannonball it captured da Castle O Muness," he answered.

I had some slight idea what a cannonball was used for but I could not see, for the life of me, how this modest lump of iron could have performed such a mighty deed. Did the attackers just threaten to fire it? If so, it did not conjure up in my brain any visions of brave defenders. Maybe the ball was fired and it caused such catastrophic damage that it compelled instant surrender.

The cannonball looked more innocuous than omnipotent but before I got any more pictures in my head my father spoke again. "Come here an al tell de what happened."

This is the story he told.

Laurence Bruce built Muness Castle in 1599. He was a mighty landowner and ruled all of Unst and much more. The castle is situated on the south-east corner of the island. He saw it as a defence against his many enemies, among them his nephew Earl Patrick Stewart who built Scalloway Castle around the same time.

They were both despotic rulers who hated each other but neither of them lasted that long. Earl Patrick was arrested and spent a number of years in prison before he was tried for treason and sentenced to death. He was beheaded in 1615.

After Laurence Bruce died, Muness Castle was occupied until 1627. This period in Shetland's history was rather lawless and many pirate ships raided settlements without much fear of serious opposition. A French privateer anchored off the south end of Unst and pirates from the ship came ashore and demanded entry to the castle.

The pirates reasoned that the castle was bound to contain valuables and they badly wanted to get their hands on any loot that was going. Entry to the castle was refused so the pirates made a show of laying siege. They declared their intention of taking the castle by force.

In fact, they regarded the castle as being too tough a nut to crack; their siege was no more than a token. They knew that if they were to take the castle it would have to be by cunning. Nonetheless, they kept up the siege for a week, but when they sailed away the defenders of the castle were delighted

Inside the castle the garrison was sure that it had seen the last of the privateer and it was cause for a great celebration. Several sheep and a pig were slaughtered and a hogshead of wine was tapped. Musicians and dancers were summonsed and a mighty party began.

It was all part of the pirates' cunning scheme. They wanted the people in the castle to believe that they had given up but, in fact, they returned under cover of darkness and landed a party of hand picked men who were heavily armed but able to move quietly in the dark.

The attackers crept as close to the castle walls as they could. They lay hidden and waited for the signal to rush the door. One of their number could speak perfect English and, dressed as a beggar, he boldly knocked on the castle door.

When he was challenged he explained that he was a poor man who had been travelling for two days without any food at all. The beautiful smell of roasting meat had driven him mad with hunger so he had knocked at the castle door to beg for a few scraps.

# The Cannonball

~ ~ ~

The effects of the wine had befuddled the guards on the door. They were in such a jolly mood that they readily agreed to take the beggar into the castle and feed him. When they opened the door the beggar took from his pocket the cannonball and jammed it into the hinge side of the door.

By the time the drunken guards had discovered the reason why the door would not shut the pirates rushed in and the castle was captured. The pirates ransacked the place and burned it down. It has been a ruin ever since.

I do not know if the cannonball I held in my hand as a boy was really the one that captured the castle, and I do not know how it came to be in the Haa of Midbrake, but I always remember the story that my father told me all those years ago.

*Many years after I first heard this story Mary Peterson gave a written version of it. Among other things it says that the capture of the castle occurred in 1627 and that the pirates set fire to it.*

# 37

# The Foy

AROUND the year 1900 a young boy from Edinburgh was in north Yell on holiday. His name was George Moar. He had very strong Shetland connections because his father was from Gloup in north Yell. His visit coincided with a time of change in the fishing industry.

For several generations the big summer effort was the haaf fishing. Fishermen would venture as far off shore as forty miles in open boats called sixtreens. As the name suggests the boats were crewed by six men; they were sailed with traditional square sails in the fashion of their forbears, the Vikings. If the wind was unfavourable the boats were rowed to and from the fishing grounds on the edge of the continental shelf.

In 1881 a terrible disaster struck the fishing fleet based at Nethertoon. On the morning of the 21st of July a sudden storm devastated the boats, six boats and thirty-six men were lost. This disaster did not end the haaf fishing entirely but it never had the same importance again.

Never again was Nethertoon in Gloup a fishing station, and the haaf fishing that lingered on in north Yell used the North Banks at the Beach of Brough, as a base. There was a lodge at the North Banks; a building where fishermen could sleep overnight. Some men lived so far away from the beach that it was impossible for them to walk home every time they came ashore.

# The Foy

~ ~ ~

Fishermen always had a foy to celebrate Johnsmas, the feast day of St John, on the 25th June and they also had a second foy at the end of each fishing season. A foy was the name they gave to a party where they ate and drank and made merry. Attending the foy at the North Banks was one of the highlights of George's holiday.

He had made friends with Dodie and John Bain, two local boys around his own age. The Bain brothers were beach boys at the North Banks. Fishermen were fishing for ling, cod and tusk and what they caught was washed, split, salted and dried and eventually exported to Catholic countries for eating on Fridays.

The Bain brothers' job was to look after the salted fish as they dried in the sun. The fish had to be turned so they dried evenly; they had to be guarded against the attempts of hungry birds to steal them, and they had to be taken inside if it began to rain.

Beach boys did not have an easy time. The work they did was highly responsible and they were paid almost nothing. They were, in effect, marking time until they were old enough to be fishermen themselves. If they had any money a favourite snack for them was a loaf of bread and a pound of roast fat that they bought from the nearby shop. The fat was roughly chopped into chunks and crunched up along with the bread. With this they might have had a mug of tea.

At the end of a fishing season – late summer, or even autumn – the men would gather at the North Banks to stow everything away for the winter to come and secure the lodge.

The boats were drawn up well away from the sea and turned upside down. They had secure places for the boats called noosts and if they were turned hull up they were far less likely to blow away during winter storms. One boat, usually a smaller boat, was kept in readiness for the sea so that any fishing opportunity during the winter could be exploited.

When all the work at the beach was done then the foy began. The beach boys and George were left in charge of the lodge and in charge of the fire and the cooking. Meanwhile, the men went to the Greenbank shop to get the drinks. The shop was an off-sales but the shop man used a back room as a place, like a pub, for his customers to drink in.

This was illegal but there were no law enforcement officers on the island at that time so the practice went on for many years. When the men were ready for their supper they bought a pig of whisky and took it back to the lodge. After a hearty supper of boiled mutton and bannocks the party got underway in earnest.

The whisky was passed around and everyone took, including the boys. In those days there was no taboo on youngsters drinking. Strong drink was so scarce that it was never seen as a danger or a threat and it was, many a time, used as medicine and given to children, so the beach boys were allowed a dram as well as the food.

There was a fiddler in the company who sat on the front of one of the stone bunks and played all the springs he knew while all the others danced. The fact that no ladies were present was no obstacle, the men danced by themselves and with each other. With only a pause for more whisky the music and dancing went on and on.

Dancing was taken very seriously and men competed to be the best and the most energetic. The event became a test of stamina. The object was to be the last one on the floor; he was then said to have "danced them all down" and he would have an extra refreshment.

By this time the older men were ready for bed but the boys still had plenty of energy and wanted to have a bit more fun. One of them got hold of a looderhorn; the large horn used at sea as a loud hailer, and began to blow it with all his might. Of course, this kept everyone from sleep and the men in bed told them in no uncertain fashion to be quiet.

To this they paid no attention but they had to go outside where they continued to make as much noise as ever. At last George Bain lost patience and got out of bed to restore order. Old Bainie, as he was sometimes known, was a giant of a man with enormous strength. He was the father of John and Dodie and he appeared outside the lodge with his bare feet and dressed only in his woollen drawers.

When he demanded that the boys hand over the looderhorn they ran a short distance and took refuge under an up-turned sixtreen and defiantly gave another blast on the horn. Old Bainie tried to squeeze under the gunwale of the boat but he was far too big so he reached in and tried to get hold of at least one of the mischief-makers.

# The Foy

~ ~ ~

They retreated to the far side and long as Bainie's arms were he could not reach the boys. He got up and walked around to the other side of the boat where the same procedure was repeated. He again demanded that the horn be given to him but this time he threatened to turn the sixtreen off them.

On the face of it this was an absurd threat; for one man to lift a sixtreen, even in a World's Strongest Man competition, would have been an awesome feat. John was well aware of the raw power of his father and he was taking no chances, without another word he surrendered the looderhorn.

When all was quiet the boys crept into the lodge and bedded themselves down and went to sleep. In the morning they came in for no punishment for their misdeeds of the previous evening. Boys will be boys, someone said, while the Bain brothers busied themselves with reviving the fire and boiling water for tea.

After breakfast George set off back to the Henderson family at the Kirks, Gloup, where he was staying. On his way he called in at Gibby Bain's shop. Mrs Henderson had asked him to bring back a reel of cotton thread. Gibby Bain was an older brother of John and Dodie, but he was very different from his giant father and robust and healthy brothers.

Gibby was, by contrast, weak and sickly. He had been born with a curved back and a large hump and he was never strong enough to do any of the usual work like crofting and fishing. At the time there was a scheme whereby boys like Gibby Bain could train for the work that they could do.

Gibby had trained as a tailor but trade, in north Yell, was limited. A man would buy a suit of clothes to get married in and that suit would be his Sunday best wear for the rest of his life. So Gibby Bain's was not just a tailor's shop but he was a general merchant as well. He also sold alcohol, on the quiet, and he was fond of a drop or two for himself.

George bought the thread and he also saw the carcase of a lamb hanging up for sale. He bought the whole shoulder of it along with two gills of whisky. The bill for his purchases came to a total of 1/10 or 8p in today's money. On the long walk back to Gloup he had time to reflect on Gibby Bain's shop and other recent events.

# The Foy and other folk tales

~ ~ ~

*In the 1950s and 60s George Moar was a frequent visitor to Gloup. In his retirement he would stay, some years, most of the summer. He had lived in Edinburgh all his life but even after sixty years his memories of north Yell were vivid and especially the foy that he attended at the North Banks.*